KISS IN THE SHADOWS

Vanessa had her dreams . . . of a house in the country that she could make into a real home for her sisters . . . of helping them to realise their own dreams of success and fame in different artistic spheres. But they could do nothing without money—and so she did not expect her dreams to be fulfilled. Yet the money came into her life unexpectedly—and with it came a proud, difficult, hostile man who resented the very existence of the Clements. Then Vanessa realised that money did not make for happiness . . . and that a kiss in the shadows was meaningless when remembered in the bright sunlight of another day.

KISS IN THE SHADOWS

Paula Lindsay

ATLANTIC LARGE PRINT

Chivers Press, Bath, England.
Curley Publishing, Inc.,
South Yarmouth, Mass., USA.

iii

Library of Congress Cataloging in Publication Data

Lindsay, Paula.
  Kiss in the shadows / Paula Lindsay.
    p.   cm.—(Atlantic large print)
  ISBN 1–55504–941–9 (lg. print)
  1. Large type books. I. Title.
  [PS3562.I511916K5 1989]
  813'.54—dc20   89–11706
                                                CIP

British Library Cataloguing in Publication Data

Lindsay, Paula, *1933*–
  Kiss in the shadows.
  I. Title
  823'.914 [F]

  ISBN 0–7451–9548–2
  ISBN 0–7451–9560–1 pbk

This Large Print edition is published by Chivers Press, England, and Curley Publishing, Inc, U.S.A. 1989

Published by arrangement with the author

U.K. Hardback ISBN 0 7451 9548 2
U.K. Softback ISBN 0 7451 9560 1
U.S.A. Softback ISBN 1 55504 941 9

KISS IN THE SHADOWS

CHAPTER ONE

The bright sunshine of the summery day barely relieved the ancient gloom of the office with its dusty bookshelves, heavy filing cabinets and furniture and drab carpeting.

Vanessa sighed and allowed her hands to drop from the keys of her typewriter. She glanced through the window at the inviting blue of the sky with its wisps of pure white cloud drifting lazily above the rooftops. She thought wistfully of a day in the country or on the coast . . . anywhere, in fact, but this stuffy office in the heart of the city.

Her corn-coloured hair matched the golden sunshine and the blue of her eyes was deeper than that of the sky. A delicate pink and white complexion, a straight and slender nose and a deliciously humourous mouth all combined to grant a fresh, appealing loveliness. A loveliness that did not pass unnoticed in a city noted for its lovely women.

Vanessa was not often discontented but she was aware of a certain restlessness, a dissatisfaction, on this lovely day as she sat idle for a few moments and ignored the sheaf of legal documents on her desk.

She was usually grateful for the good job with its adequate salary and reasonable

1

working conditions and she found the work itself interesting enough. But the sunshine and unusually warm weather evoked a feeling of rebellion and she began to dream of all the enjoyable things she might be doing with the day if she was not compelled to earn her living as a secretary.

Wandering through fields and lanes, communing with trees and birds and tiny brooks and wild squirrels . . . basking in the warmth of the sun, as free as the air, asking nothing but a sandwich and a flask of tea and the thought of long hours with nothing to do but enjoy herself. Driving in an open car with the wind in her hair, heading for a quiet coastal bay with the thought of golden sands and sparkling sea and the distant sound of children at play. Sitting in a deckchair on a very green lawn with an iced drink in her hand, her sisters sprawled on the grass at her feet, soft music in the background and an inviting pool awaiting their pleasure.

She came abruptly back to reality as the telephone shrilled and she was forced to thrust those pleasant pictures from her mind.

Having dealt with the call, she turned back to her typewriter and soon her fingers were moving rapidly over the keys. Dreams were all very well but her kind of dreams needed money to make them reality—and money was the one gift that the fairies had failed to bring to her christening! She and her sisters had sufficient for their needs . . . to pay the rent of their flat, to feed and clothe themselves, to indulge in the occasional extravagance, to pay for the annual holiday and to put aside a little each week in case of emergency.

Vanessa reminded herself that she was really very fortunate. She had a good job, a roof over her head and the affection and company of her sisters. Life would have been much, much worse if she had been an only child! Also, she had friends in plenty and life was never dull. It was foolish and futile to hanker for things she might never have—and she would probably be very bored indeed if she had enough money to do nothing but laze about all day and every day . . .

Philip Hennessy, a junior partner in the firm, came into the room to return a book to the shelves. Then he perched on the edge of Vanessa's desk and smiled down at her.

'I don't feel a bit like work,' he mourned. 'Don't you wish you could put on your hat and walk out? We could spend the day on the river—or somewhere equally cool and pleasant.'

'If wishes were horses beggars would ride,' she retorted lightly, typed the last word on the sheet and took it from her typewriter.

'Don't be so prosaic,' he rebuked. 'Anyway, beggars are almost non-existent in this Welfare State—most of them are driving about in cars maintained by the National

Assistance!'

'If that's true then I must be mad to work for my living! I can't think of anything nicer than driving somewhere lovely on a day like this.'

'There's always the weekend,' he said quickly. 'The weather should hold until Monday at least, according to the experts. Let me take you down to the coast? We could have a good time.'

'Thank you . . . but I have other arrangements for Sunday, I'm afraid.'

'Did I suggest Sunday? Why not Saturday then?'

'That isn't possible either,' she told him, managing to introduce just the right amount of rue into her tone.

'What a popular young woman you are,' he mocked. 'I wonder what all your other admirers have that I haven't?' He shook his head in mock wonder. 'It can't be persistence—I've been trying to date you for the last six months without success. You know, you're much too lovely to be wasted in this dump, Vanessa. Why on earth do you stick it? With your face and figure you could make the most of the opportunities that must come your way. I wonder what you'd really do with your life if you had the chance?'

She was too inured to his idle compliments to feel more than a momentary gratification. She gave a little shrug. 'Oh, I don't know . . .

4

waste it, probably, doing nothing.'

'Sounds bliss.' He produced his cigarette case and, as Vanessa shook her head to the offer, helped himself to a cigarette. 'Will you have lunch with me? We could play truant this afternoon—drive to Richmond and take a boat on the river.'

'Very tempting—but quite out of the question.' She inserted a virgin sheet of paper into her typewriter.

'Richmond—or lunch?'

'Both,' she said firmly and pointedly began to type.

'Busy little bee, aren't you?'

'Very busy,' she agreed crisply.

'Oh, I can take a hint.' He straightened and strode to the door. 'You know, my sweet, the conscientious types usually end up as conscientious old maids—surely you don't want that to happen to you?'

'I can think of worse fates,' she retorted blithely . . . and sighed with relief as the door closed behind him. Philip Hennessy was much too handsome for his own good—and his evident conviction that every girl would fall over herself to be noticed by him had always irritated Vanessa. He was attractive and amusing and she liked him—but she had no intention of encouraging his attempts at flirtation. She did not mean to be one more name on the list of his conquests—and he made no secret of the fact that he was not a marrying man.

It would be very easy to accept one of his many invitations and no doubt she would enjoy an evening in his company . . . but an affair with Philip, however innocent, could promise no future. Vanessa was not unduly anxious to be married but at the same time she did not want to drift from one affair to another with men who were merely passing attractions.

In any case, it was never wise to mix business with pleasure and old Mr. Hardy, the head of the firm and her immediate employer, was fast losing patience with Philip because of his outrageous flirtations with every woman on the staff, regardless of looks or age or eligibility. He was never to be taken seriously and Vanessa did not want to become embroiled in the inevitable showdown.

She allowed Philip to believe that she was much in demand by other men because it was the easiest way of brushing off his invitations. But it was very far from the truth if Philip imagined that all her free time was taken up by men friends. She had occasional dates, of course—and until recently there had been one regular escort. But the emphasis was always on friendship and she had earned herself a reputation as a cool, touch-me-not type—and this suited her very well. One day the only man would come into her life . . . she did not want a long list of trivial affairs to her credit

6

when that day dawned. In the meantime, surely it was possible to go to a theatre or a cinema or a party with a man without having to 'pay' for one's evening by suffering unwelcome attentions at the end of it. So far she had contrived to keep every man at arm's length and it would not be her fault if she did not continue to do so until the one man she could care for came over the hill!

By sharing a flat with her sisters, she was automatically provided with an easy escape if any man proved difficult to handle. A faint smile touched her lips at the thought that one day she might resent the lack of privacy and wish her sisters a thousand miles away when she was escorted home after an evening out. Certainly Belinda grumbled enough and threatened to find a flat of her own . . . but Vanessa privately thought it all to the good that her younger sister did not have the privacy she demanded. She was young and headstrong and impulsive and a little silly—and not all of her escorts were the type that could be left alone with a young girl with impunity.

The door was pushed open and Maureen, the junior typist who shared the office, came in with a tray. 'The wolf been prowling about again?' she asked as she placed a cup of steaming, fragrant coffee on Vanessa's desk.

'Mr. Hennessy came to return a book.' But Vanessa smiled.

'Any excuse serves . . . especially when he knows that I'm out of the way. He never gives up, does he?' Maureen sat down at her own desk, pulled open a drawer and took a powder compact from her bag. She busied herself with renewing the make-up which might have suffered during the arduous task of making and taking round the coffee.

Vanessa lighted a cigarette and watched her idly, glad of the ten-minute break in the middle of a busy morning. 'How's Stan?' she asked, more to provide the other girl with the pleasure of talking about her fiancé than because she continued to feel any curiosity about the young man.

'Smashing! We went to look at a flat last night . . . one of his mates told him about it. Four quid a week and a meter for the gas. Daylight robbery.'

'Never mind, Maureen. You'll find something soon,' Vanessa soothed.

'Oh, we took it. Case of Hobson's choice these days, isn't it? It's not a bad place and Stan and his mates will decorate it. It's better than living with his Mum, anyway. I thought it might come to that with only a month before the wedding. Oh, she'd be delighted to have her darling boy stay in the nest and feed him up with hot dinners and darn his socks. But I'm not having that,' she went on hotly. 'I can cook as well as his Mum can—and who needs to darn socks when I can buy him nylon ones and make sure he cuts his toe-nails!'

Vanessa hastily smothered a smile. Maureen's pert, matter-of-fact approach to life always amused her and she sincerely wished the girl every happiness with her Stan. Having heard a great deal about Stan and Stan's Mum during the last few months and knowing Maureen so well, she was pretty certain that Maureen would defeat the older woman in any battle of wits . . . and end up as a younger, slightly more modern copy of Stan's Mum in due course.

'So you'll be looking at furniture now, I suppose?'

Maureen nodded happily. 'I've seen a lovely suite . . . black leather with bright red cushions. I'm going to have matching red curtains and a peacock blue carpet. And one of those modern breakfast sets in the kitchen and a lovely set of units. It'll be smashing.'

'You must have been saving up like mad.'

'We've enough for the deposits . . . we'll have it all on H.P., of course. Stan's Mum wants to buy us a bedroom suite for a wedding present . . . I told him that's okay but I'm choosing it. I know her taste—and it isn't mine!'

'It's a very generous present,' Vanessa said.

'Oh, she's not a bad old girl. We'll get along fine as long as she doesn't interfere—and I'll be glad of her to take care of the kids later on while I go back to work. Oh, well, speaking of work . . .' she added with a glance at the wall clock. 'Just think, Van . . . this time next month I'll be on my honeymoon—laying on the beach in my bikini and thinking of you slogging away at that rotten old typewriter.'

She almost danced from the room with the tray and the empty cups and Vanessa looked after her with an indulgent smile. She almost envied the eighteen-year-old girl's happy dream of the future. She also admired the easy, unquestioning acceptance of a marriage which demanded that she should continue to work and run her home and look after her husband until she had a child—and then probably return to work as soon as the child was old enough to be handed over to the care of Stan's Mum. Vanessa appreciated the necessity if Stan and Maureen were to fulfil their dream of a house of their own one day but she doubted if she could face such a future with equanimity and wondered if she was made of such stern stuff as Maureen.

She did not want to spend the rest of her life in an office. Like any other young woman, she had dreams of a husband, home and family. But she did not want to marry and live in furnished rooms and struggle to pay the rent and dread the prospect of having a child before they could afford it and see their dream of their own house fading into

10

thin air. It happened to so many young couples and they seemed to find their happiness despite the difficulties—but the thought of such a future for herself horrified Vanessa.

Money . . . or rather the lack of it . . . was at the bottom of everything. What did one do to get money in this world . . . enough money to provide the luxuries that one would like, enough money to ensure security and comfort and peace of mind, enough money to buy all the things one wanted—without working for it? Some girls married money—but Vanessa shrank from the thought of marrying solely for the sake of a bank balance. And it seemed too much to hope for that the one man for whom she waited would not only love her but would also be able to keep her in the luxury she could so easily become accustomed to!

There had never been much money . . . partly because her father's work as an artist had never been appreciated by anyone but family and friends, partly because five children to feed and clothe had been a constant drain on the family purse, partly because her mother had never learned economy and had been woefully extravagant in many ways.

Once she had remarked ruefully that it was not easy to lose the habit of spending money like water—a remark that had brought a torrent of curious questions that had never

11

been answered. Now, as Vanessa pondered the age-old problem of money and its lack, she wondered if her mother's family had once been wealthy. She and her sisters had never been told anything about that family and they had automatically assumed that their mother had no family.

Vanessa wondered why money had suddenly become so important. It couldn't be just the bright sunshine and her dissatisfaction with her job. Was it Maureen's bright, blindly-trusting talk of a future with her Stan—and the crystallisation in Vanessa's mind of the knowledge that a similar future was probably in store for her?

Was it Rowena's desperate dream of being an artist—and the knowledge that it could never be anything but a dream while there was insufficient money to provide her with security while she tried to make a name for herself. She was working in an art gallery and her kindly employer allowed her to display her canvases among the others for sale and she sold the occasional painting . . . but she longed to go to a good art school.

Was it Fiona's ardent wish to open her own dress salon and to design beautiful clothes in beautiful materials—and the knowledge that she was saving every penny towards the fulfilment of that dream while she worked as a saleswoman in a Kensington gown shop?

Was it Belinda with her ambition to be a

12

famous actress and move in exalted circles and who had to be content with a poorly-paid job as a very junior member of a third-rate repertory company? No one could doubt that Belinda would get what she wanted in time but it was a long way to the West End and her name in lights from a small suburban theatre that was always on the verge of closing down—and Vanessa dreaded that the impatient girl would take a dubious route to the top if her eager hands could not grasp all she wanted by legitimate means.

Was it Melissa and her music? Her longing for a piano and endless hours in which to practise and teaching by the masters and the culmination of it all on the concert platform? At the moment she thanked the good fortune which had provided the friendly interest of old Mr. Rawley and the use of his piano—but she did not have much time to take advantage of his offer, working as a nanny to the old man's grandchildren as she did.

If a vast sum of money were to drop unexpectedly into Vanessa's lap, she could give each of her sisters her heart's desire and feel that the money was being put to good use. For herself, she would ask nothing except freedom from the daily monotony of an office job and a nice little house in the country where she could make a home for her sisters. But such things did not happen outside fiction and the glamorous, unlikely world of film productions—and Vanessa could only hope that they might fulfil their separate dreams before they were too old or too apathetic . . .

Checking her wandering thoughts, she diligently applied herself to the typewriter. It would not help matters if she day-dreamed herself out of a job!

The day was very long and the office grew stuffier and stuffier despite the open window. Vanessa thought ruefully that it was typical of the English climate to throw a heat wave in the middle of May . . . they could certainly expect a wet and dreary summer to follow.

As the hands of the clock moved towards five, she began to tidy her desk and look forward to the evening—and stifled the thought of a crowded and uncomfortable train journey which was the necessary penance at the end of the working day.

Maureen left promptly with a swirl of her gaily-coloured skirts and Vanessa did not pause to do more than slip on her light coat, ram her hat on her bright curls and grant the room a cursory last glance before leaving.

Philip Hennessy was passing the door and delayed her with the suggestion that they should have coffee together and then he would run her home in his car. She thanked him but refused on the plea that her sisters would be anxious if she were late. As she mingled with the surging crowd in the street,

Vanessa promptly forgot all about Philip and her mind turned to the problem of arriving home in one piece and in time to have the kettle boiling and the evening meal prepared before her sisters came in from work.

CHAPTER TWO

The Clements considered themselves lucky to have found the flat which was the top half of a big, older-type house—even at the rental of ten guineas a week. Two guineas apiece had not seemed exorbitant for a pleasant and comfortable home where they could be together.

Vanessa was a natural home-maker and it was she who had found the flat, supervised the move and arranged the furnishings, bought material for curtains and chair-covers and painstakingly sewn them by hand and agreed to take care of the catering if the others would pull their weight in the care of the flat.

Her sisters did not mean to be selfish or thoughtless—but each of them had a demanding interest and thus most of the housework as well as the cooking and shopping fell to Vanessa's lot. She took pride in keeping the flat clean and attractive and much of her time was taken in polishing and sweeping, washing and ironing and the thousand and one things that go into the making of a home.

The others protested—but the protests were half-hearted . . . and then Rowena would return to her canvas and paints, Fiona would bend her head over her sketch book, Melissa would take herself and her yearning fingers over the road to Mr. Rawley's piano and Belinda would grumble and groan and tear her hair over her part for the next production—during those weeks when she was not appearing at the theatre. And Vanessa would smile indulgently and carry on with the self-set tasks that were also her pleasure.

When their mother died and the girls realised that they had no one but each other, Vanessa had determined to make a home for her sisters and do all she could to keep them together. It would have been easy for them to drift apart, even to lose touch in time, each following their separate dreams. Vanessa hoped that only marriage would break up the close-knit family group—and knew that because it was a happy home without restrictions not one of her sisters would hurry into marriage simply to be free of the boredom and loneliness of a bed-sitter which was the fate of so many who lived and worked in the big city.

As Vanessa had hoped, the kettle was

boiling and the evening meal was well under way when steps on the stairs announced the arrival of one of her sisters.

Belinda came in and tossed her bag on the newly-laid table. 'What a day! I must have been mad to go down on my knees to Benjamin for a job! I'd like to poison his next cup of coffee—and if he doesn't lay off me I swear I will!'

She was the youngest, as dark as Vanessa was fair, her long, raven hair piled high and dark eyes dancing with merriment, glowing with all the youth and vitality of an eighteen-year-old who is doing what she wants to do with her life.

Vanessa quietly transferred the bag to a chair and gave her sister a sympathetic smile. 'Bad rehearsal? Never mind—you won't be with the Benjamin Players for ever and it's very good experience, after all.'

Belinda snorted. 'It might be if Benjamin ever gave me a decent part. I'm getting fed-up with walk-ons and dumb maids!'

'Of course you are but you've only been with them for four months. Better parts will come in time.'

'Every actress has to prove her worth, Miss Clement,' Belinda said in bitter mimicry of her employer. 'How can I when he never gives me a chance. Anyone could play a maid's part!'

Vanessa smiled. 'I couldn't.'

Belinda swept on indignantly: 'Why does he have to constantly remind me that I'm the most junior and least necessary member of the cast? He's the most tyrannical, pigheaded, conceited man I've ever met in my life.' Her mood changed abruptly as it was apt to do. 'Oh, well, no good grumbling . . . I chose the life, after all. How was your day?'

'Hot and dull.'

'It was awful in the theatre—absolutely stifling,' Belinda went on, scarcely noticing that Vanessa had replied. 'Thank heavens I'm not working tonight. I mean to have a bath and enjoy a thoroughly lazy evening . . .'

'That sounds in character!' Fiona exclaimed lightly, catching the tail end of Belinda's remark. She smiled at Vanessa affectionately. 'Just what *you* need, ducky—you look washed out,' she commented with all the frankness of a sister.

Vanessa shrugged. 'It was rather a trying day, that's all.' She went into the kitchen.

Fiona threw herself into a deep, comfortable arm-chair and took a cigarette from her case. 'Heaven!' she murmured, thankfully relaxing after the long, tiring day. The bright sunshine had brought a flock of customers in search of summer clothes and many of them, already made irritable by the warmth of the day, had been more than difficult to please.

'What's to eat?' she demanded as Vanessa

18

returned with a bowl of cool, inviting salad.

'Nothing very exciting . . . only lamb chops and green salad and cold trifle to follow.'

'It sounds delicious,' said Belinda. 'I don't know how you do it . . . were you home early?'

'No. I prepared the salad this morning and bought the chops on my way home,' she explained, as voices on the stairs announced the arrival of the rest of the family.

Rowena and Melissa came in together. Barely a year separated their ages and they were enough alike to be often mistaken for twins. Both girls were fair-haired and fair-skinned, remarkably pretty and with the same grey, grave eyes fringed by long, dark lashes. Like Vanessa, they had inherited their fairness from their mother: Fiona and Belinda were both as dark as their father had been.

'Just look at the ladies of leisure—hogging the armchairs while Van does everything, as usual!' Melissa scoffed.

'Van isn't on her feet all day coping with beastly women who have more money than sense and insist on wearing the most unsuitable clothes,' Fiona retorted lazily.

'And what's your excuse?' Rowena turned to Belinda.

'As the youngest and the spoiled brat of the family, she doesn't need one,' Fiona retorted while Belinda merely grinned.

'Very true,' she agreed complacently. 'Besides, I have to conserve my energy for my star-studded career.'

The grumbles and the highlights of the day were the main topic of conversation while they ate and only Vanessa did not contribute for she was too busy plying them with food and listening to their comments and no one thought to ask about her day. She knew that it was generally accepted that her job was easy, pleasant and undemanding and she had never tried to disillusion them.

It was a full-time job looking after her sisters in one way and another and often Vanessa marvelled that she had any time left for herself. She was maid to each of them in turn and sometimes to two of them at the same time: ensuring that dresses were pressed and laid out in readiness for an evening out, running the bath and mopping up afterwards, putting a timely stitch into a bra strap and sorting out a perfect pair of stockings from the motley assortment stuffed into a drawer, finding the missing articles that her sisters could never find for themselves, assisting with the actual preparation for the date and then abruptly left to tidy up the resulting upheaval.

Vanessa was one of those rare people who delight in being used by whoever might need them at any given moment. She would not have changed her sisters in any way—and certainly she was so used to their ways that she would never dream of describing them as selfish or lazy or thoughtless. Their evident affection, their unspoken gratitude for all she did, their confident conviction that Vanessa would always come when called were all that she asked and she was quite content . . . except for those occasional moments when she longed to be able to give her sisters all that they wanted.

She knew, of course, that a fortune would not drop into her lap from the skies so she wisely pushed her day-dreams to the back of her mind and got on with life as it was.

The meal over, she cleared the table and ran hot water into the sink for the washing-up. Belinda lounged against the kitchen table and watched her idly. It did not occur to her to lend a hand and neither did it occur to Vanessa to suggest that she should. She was much too intent on finishing the task before Fiona shouted for assistance. For Fiona was going out that evening with her current escort: Rowena and Melissa were going to a party; and all three of them would have her running round in circles, she thought with wry amusement.

'Not going out?' Belinda asked.

'Not tonight.'

'Oh . . . I've asked some of the gang to come. You don't mind, do you?'

'Why should I? It's your home,' Vanessa

replied evenly but she felt a prickle of irritation that Belinda never failed to tell her these things at the last moment.

'You'll rustle up some sandwiches, won't you?'

Vanessa frowned briefly. 'I haven't anything exciting to give them—they'll have to take cheese and corned beef and like it.'

'Oh, don't worry . . . that'll be all right . . . unless you run round to the delicatessen and get some salami and some soused herrings and sauerkraut and some of those lovely little rolls.'

Vanessa concentrated furiously on a dirty plate so that Belinda should not see the tide of angry colour which had stormed her cheeks. She did not mind Belinda inviting her friends to the flat but she certainly drew the line at 'running round to the delicatessen' for special food for them when she had so much to do . . . and little money left to last till the end of the week. If Belinda objected to giving her friends cheese and corned beef sandwiches then it was up to her to go to the delicatessen and provide for them!

The silence dragged for a minute or two. Then Belinda said sulkily: 'Oh, never mind—I don't suppose they'll care what they eat, anyway. I'd better go and drag Fiona out of the bathroom—she never seems to realise that other people might want to get ready for the evening.'

Vanessa was thankful to be alone for a few moments. She was shocked and horrified at the anger which had flared to life. Any other evening, she would have agreed to Belinda's suggestion without hesitation—and dropped whatever she might be doing to ensure the success of Belinda's evening. But rebellion had caught her by surprise. She knew that Belinda was cross and disappointed . . . but not enough concerned to go to the delicatessen herself. She would soon get over her sulkiness and promptly forget Vanessa's lack of co-operation.

Melissa put her head into the kitchen. 'I've borrowed your blue evening shoes—you don't mind, do you?'

Vanessa swung round impatiently. 'Yes, I do mind! They're brand-new and I haven't worn them myself yet! What's wrong with your own evening shoes?'

'The buckle's off . . . I *told* you! Don't be mean, Van . . . I won't hurt your precious shoes. They're perfect with this dress—look!' And she pirouetted around the kitchen, her eyes full of coaxing, her most winning smile in full play.

'I stitched the buckle on the other night and your own shoes will look just as nice with that dress,' Vanessa said firmly.

Melissa stopped abruptly. 'Did you?' Her eyes widened. 'But how could you? I lost the buckle.'

'I went to Oxford Street one lunch hour and bought a new pair—they're much nicer than the old ones. I suppose you haven't even looked!' she accused, half-impatient, half-amused.

'You are an angel, Van . . . how much do I owe you for the buckles?'

'Call it a Christmas present,' she returned with a faint smile, stacking the last dish in the draining rack and turning to wipe down the cooker.

Melissa danced away and Vanessa winced, thinking of her elegant new shoes and her sister's notorious clumsiness. She was quite likely to slip on the few stairs that led down to the bedrooms and break the heel. Vanessa strained her ears for the half-expected thud of her fall—and sighed with relief as it never came.

The next moment she hurried in Melissa's wake at the sound of Fiona's call—and found her sister wrapped in a bath-towel and pulling everything out of the chest of drawers.

'What on earth are you looking for?' Vanessa demanded, stooping to retrieve the fallen under-garments.

'My new nylon under-set—I can't think what's happened to it! If one of these wretches has borrowed it . . .'

Vanessa indicated to a froth of nylon and lace that lay over the bed. 'This?'

Fiona had the grace to look sheepish.

'Trust me to wander round wth my eyes closed . . . thanks, Van. Are you busy? Would you transfer my things to my evening bag? Not all the junk, of course . . . purse, keys, comb . . . the usual things.'

Rowena wandered into the room. She wore nothing but the flimsiest of underthings and her long fair hair tumbled past her shoulders. 'Van, can I borrow that peachy lipstick again? I forgot to get one in my lunch hour.'

Vanessa opened the drawer which contained her own cosmetics—its neatness and cleanliness in striking contrast to the hotch-potch of Fiona's cosmetics which had been turned out in a heap on top of the dressing-table.

She handed the lipstick to Rowena. 'You can have it,' she said lightly. 'It's easier to get a new one for myself.'

'But this is almost new!'

Vanessa laughed. 'Then you're not losing anything, are you?'

Forgetting to thank her, Rowena returned to the bedroom she shared with Melissa and Belinda. Fiona raised an eyebrow. 'You are an idiot,' she said bluntly. 'She'll have that lipstick about a week before she loses it—and then she'll be round you again to borrow your new one.'

Vanessa shrugged. 'It's one of the penalties for having the same colouring as one's sisters.'

25

'Don't include me,' Fiona said lazily, leaning closer to the mirror as she plucked at a stray eyebrow hair. 'Just thank your lucky stars that at least I can't wear your make-up.'

'No . . . just my clothes,' Vanessa retorted teasingly. 'Sometimes I wish I were six feet tall and as wide as a house so I'd be the only one to wear my things.'

'Don't forget that you can also wear my clothes,' Fiona said, conveniently ignoring the undeniable truth that Vanessa never did borrow any of her possessions . . . and mildly wondering that this sister should be so different to the others in so many ways. She began to make up her face, carefully and expertly. 'You know, you do too much for those girls. You shouldn't wait on them hand and foot like you do . . . pass that eyeshadow, would you . . . oh, help, is that the time? I'm going to be late . . . I feel it in my bones. Be an angel and start on my hair while you're standing there with nothing to do.' Vanessa obediently picked up a brush and began to build up the thick dark hair into the sophisticated style that Fiona affected. Fiona went on impatiently: 'You could work your fingers to the bone for those lazy, thoughtless kids and not a word of thanks from any of them. You know, you really have a flair for hairdressing—I wonder you never thought of taking it up, Van.' Without a pause she swept on with her scolding: 'You might enjoy being

26

"little mother" but it doesn't leave you much time to live your own life, does it? When did you last have a date, for instance?'

Amusement quirked Vanessa's mouth as she busied herself with her sister's hair and listened in silence to the diatribe. Dear Fiona . . . censuring her sisters in all unconsciousness that she was equally guilty of taking Vanessa for granted.

'You know perfectly well that I went to a concert last Tuesday,' she replied serenely.

'Heavens, yes—and what a to-do there was to get you off in time to meet David! All because you would wash up and hear Belinda's lines and then fuss over Melissa's dress before making any move to get ready. That's exactly what I mean . . . it's about time you began to think about yourself and left the girls to fend more for themselves.'

It was all Vanessa could do to stem the sharp retort that the washing-up would have been waiting when she returned from her evening with David; that it was quicker and easier to hear Belinda's lines than to cope with a sulky girl who might throw a panicky tantrum at any minute; that Fiona herself might have helped by taking up the hem of Melissa's new dress if she had not been so preoccupied with persuading Vanessa to telephone a man-friend and cry off a date because she had stupidly forgotten it and double-dated herself.

Vanessa had been late and David had been furious and torn up the concert tickets in a fit of childish temper and the entire evening had been ruined. He had not telephoned since that evening and she did not really expect to hear from him again. She had liked David but his sulkiness and selfishness had reminded her too much of Belinda . . . forgivable in a girl of eighteen but intolerable in a man of thirty-odd.

Fiona was irritated by her sister's silence but was opportunely distracted as she gave the final touch to the newly-dressed hair by spraying it with lacquer.

'Lovely,' she approved. 'No one does my hair like you, Van. If I every marry a millionaire I'll have you for my personal maid.' She rose to slip into the ivory-coloured dress which lay waiting for her.

Vanessa hurried from the room and went to see if the younger girls needed her assistance. But both were ready and had managed perfectly well . . . which did not prevent them grumbling because Fiona had commandeered so much of her time.

At last, the flat was comparatively peaceful and Vanessa stood at the window to watch Fiona step into her escort's car—and wondered at her sister's talent for attracting men who invariably owned expensive cars and could afford nightclubs, theatre stalls and the most lavish and sophisticated restaurants.

Then, smiling at herself for a tiny prick of envy, she turned away and began to help Belinda with the moving of the furniture to allow plenty of room for dancing when her friends arrived . . .

Belinda's party did not break up until midnight and then Vanessa sent the yawning girl to her bed and cleared away the evidence of a riotous evening. She had scarcely finished when Rowena and Melissa burst in on a tumult of excited laughter. She made them hot drinks and listened patiently to their account of the party, successfully concealing her weariness. Before she could pack them off to bed, Fiona returned home in a mood as black as thunder and treated them all to a heated diatribe on the treachery and conceit of men . . . having discovered that her escort had borrowed the expensive car belonging to his employer, that he was a chauffeur in wolf's clothing and that his idea of a gay night out was a visit to the local Palais, coffee and hamburgers in a revolting little café followed by a no holds barred wrestling bout in a cul-de-sac!

Vanessa, sympathising with her disappointment, was quite unable to stifle her laughter—and as though waiting for the cue both Melissa and Rowena collapsed into giggles. Fortunately, Fiona's own sense of humour defeated her bad temper . . . but it was still almost two o'clock before Vanessa crept between the sheets.

CHAPTER THREE

Fiona pushed away her empty cup, yawned mightily and turned to the small pile of letters beside her place. Meanwhile, Vanessa was occupied in the wild scramble to get the others off to work. She was always the last to leave and she liked to prepare for the evening meal as much as possible before hurrying off to catch the bus and tube train to the City.

'How odd!' Fiona exclaimed abruptly.

Busily clearing the table, Vanessa scarcely heeded the exclamation. She glanced briefly at Fiona who was studying a typewritten letter with a slight frown creasing her brow.

'How *very* odd!' Fiona's exclamation was more emphatic this time and Vanessa could scarcely ignore the pointed insistence on her attention.

'Is anything wrong?' she asked, pausing in her task but managing to convey her reluctance to leave what she was doing.

Fiona reached for her cigarette case. 'It's a letter from your firm . . . I suppose you didn't type it, Van? Is it some kind of practical joke?'

'What are you talking about?' Vanessa demanded with some impatience.

30

Fiona tossed the letter across the table. 'This!'

Vanessa picked up the single sheet and read it through, frowning just as Fiona had done. 'I don't know anything about it,' she said slowly, puzzled.

Fiona shrugged. 'Nor do I! How fascinating! Who on earth is Sir Wilfrid Fairgarth, anyway . . . something to my advantage—that's usually money in their jargon, isn't it? You should know, Van.'

Vanessa smiled and quipped lightly: 'I expect it's one of your erstwhile admirers.'

'But I've never heard of the man!'

'Oh, you've probably forgotten his name, that's all. It wouldn't be the first time,' she retorted teasingly.

'They must mean me, I suppose?'

'It's addressed to Miss Fiona Clement,' Vanessa pointed out.

'Well, I haven't the time to traipse across the City to see your Mr. Hardy, my dear—and it would be pretty pointless when you're actually on the spot. Find out what it's all about for me, sweetie—I must fly . . . I daren't be late again this week.' She hastily stubbed her cigarette, rose from the table and caught up her coat. 'This impossible weather!' she grumbled. 'I suppose it will pour with rain when I take my holiday.'

'Wait a minute, Fiona . . . you really must see Mr. Hardy yourself . . .' But she was

31

talking to thin air for with a kiss of her finger-tips Fiona had rushed from the room and clattered down the staircase.

Vanessa sat down and read the letter again, ignoring the partially-cleared table, the jobs she had assigned herself and the necessity to get herself ready for the day's work.

It was the type of letter that she had typed out hundreds of times since she had worked for Hardy and Bamber, Solicitors. But this one had not passed through her hands—and Maureen, with her head filled with wedding plans, had probably not even noticed the similarity of name and address. Dealing with the estate of the late Sir Wilfrid Fairgarth, it requested Miss Fiona Clement to contact the above solicitors at her earliest convenience when she would learn something to her advantage . . .

It was all very mysterious and rather exciting—how wonderful if an unexpected windfall had come Fiona's way . . . perhaps enough to enable her to fulfil her dream of her own dress shop! It was not surprising that the name of Sir Wilfrid Fairgarth had left Fiona unmoved—she had known so many different men and turned down a dozen proposals of marriage and her memory for names had always been bad.

Vanessa wondered if Mr. Hardy would divulge the advantageous something to her even if she provided satisfactory proof that she was Fiona's sister. He was rather a stickler for doing things properly—and he would be most annoyed if Vanessa hinted that Fiona had not been interested enough to follow up the polite request in the letter. But she might learn enough from the files to persuade Fiona that she would be silly to ignore Mr. Hardy's request.

Day-dreaming, hoping against hope that the mysterious legacy would be something worth having, she allowed the minutes to slip by . . . and then, horrified, scrambled into her coat and left everything to battle with the crowds and eventually reach the cool, dark office.

Maureen looked up as she entered. 'I thought it would never happen!' she exclaimed.

Vanessa took off her coat and gave herself a cursory glance in the mirror. 'Thought what would never happen?'

'You being late! Ten minutes—and it's the first time I've ever been here before you!' The triumphant note tickled Vanessa's sense of humour and she laughed.

'Late night,' she offered in explanation. 'Is Mr. Hardy in yet?'

'Not yet . . . aren't you lucky?'

'Oh, I don't suppose it would have meant the sack,' she retorted lightly. She skimmed quickly through the pile of letters on her desk and then began the task of sorting them into categories. Taking the hint, Maureen inserted a sheet into her typewriter and drew a file towards her. The morning's work had begun . . .

The intercom buzzed just after ten o'clock and Vanessa picked up notebook and newly-sharpened pencil and went to answer the summons.

The white-haired solicitor was sitting at his desk, his hands poised so that finger-tips barely touched, his head slightly inclined towards his client in a seemingly gracious gesture that strove to conceal a growing deafness.

Vanessa slipped into a seat and waited.

'You seem to be taking the devil of a time over this business . . .'

'Ah, but we have traced the young lady and written to her only this week,' Mr. Hardy interrupted smoothly and soothingly, ignoring the vehement rudeness of the younger man's attitude.

'I shouldn't have thought that it would take you three months to trace the girl,' he returned bluntly.

'There were difficulties ' . . . if you remember, we were trying to find her mother and it was not until we learned of her unfortunate demise that we turned our attention to the young lady.'

He moved restlessly and Vanessa received the impression of sudden impatience with the solicitor's pomposity.

'It was mere chance that elicited the information that Miss Clement was occupying a flat in Streatham . . .'

Vanessa half-rose to her feet, swift colour rushing to her face, the striking coincidence almost over-whelming her. 'Mr. Hardy . . .'

He quelled her with a forbidding glance. 'I won't keep you a moment, Miss Clement . . .' He broke off with raised eyebrows, realising for the first time the similarity in names.

The client was not slow to grasp the coincidence. 'Not Fiona Clement, by any chance?' he asked drily, swinging in his seat to address Vanessa. 'That would be too ridiculous—searching the whole of London for somebody actually under one's office roof.' There was a scathing insolence in his tone which hinted that it was no more than he had expected from a dry-as-dust solicitor who should have retired a decade before!

'No . . . not Fiona,' she said hastily. 'I'm Vanessa Clement.'

'Then we needn't waste any more time,' he said crisply and turned back to the solicitor.

Vanessa felt rebuffed but determinedly approached the desk. Rude and arrogant though he might be, he obviously had some connection with the matter that involved Fiona—and it was equally obvious that they had been discussing the matter.

'Fiona Clement is my sister,' she said firmly. 'She received a letter from you this morning, Mr. Hardy and . . . and wondered if it would be possible for you to divulge the information to me.'

'Really, Miss Clement . . . what you suggest is most unorthodox and quite out of the question,' Mr. Hardy said testily. 'You know that perfectly well and I'm surprised that you should imagine that the letter of the law can be bypassed in such a manner.'

'I imagine you can prove that Fiona Clement is your sister.' The younger man looked up at her with a sardonic lift of his eyebrow and made his comment as though the solicitor had not spoken.

'Why, yes, of course!'

'Have you ever heard of Ulric Clement?' he fired at her abruptly.

Taken aback, disliking his imperious tone, Vanessa threw him a cool, haughty glance which should have done more than slide so easily over him. 'My father,' she said coldly.

'You can prove that too—your sister and yourself?'

'Naturally.' Ice hovered on her lips.

A faint, sardonic smile quivered at the corners of his mouth. 'Good. Well, Mr. Hardy, truth is certainly stranger than fiction . . . three months to find Fiona Clement and three minutes to discover her sister is in your employ?'

'I had no reason to suspect any such connection,' Mr. Hardy said crossly and sent Vanessa a hostile glance as though she were entirely to blame for the long delay.

'Have you any proof of your relationship to Fiona Clement with you at the moment?' the client demanded.

'I have the letter that Fiona received from Mr. Hardy this morning,' she said uncertainly. Then with a sudden tilt to her chin, she added bitingly: 'I'm afraid I'm not in the habit of carrying my birth certificate about with me.'

'Somerset House is a mere ten minutes' walk away,' he said drily. 'But I don't think that will be necessary—birth certificates can be produced later. I suppose you know that your mother's name was Fairgarth before she married a so-called artist by the name of Clement?'

Vanessa could have kicked herself for not realising earlier why the name of Fairgarth should strike a familiar chord in her mind. 'I knew . . . but I'd forgotten,' she admitted honestly.

'Indeed?' His tone was sceptical. 'Then you had also forgotten that Sir Wilfrid was your uncle?'

'I've never heard of him before today,' she said firmly.

'Incredible,' he murmured.

'It's perfectly true,' she said hotly.

Mr. Hardy tried to interpose, disliking the feeling that he had been relegated to the background and that this aggressive young man was conducting an interview with his secretary as though everything was in his hands . . . which it was, virtually. Hardy and Bamber had merely been asked to trace the sister and/or children of Sir Wilfrid Fairgarth—their client had stipulated that he should deal with the matter once Jane Clement or her eldest child had been in touch with the solicitors. 'I still think that Miss Fiona Clement should be present before anything is divulged, Mr. Fairgarth . . .'

'More waste of time? No, I'm quite prepared to explain the business to this Miss Clement.' He rose to his feet, a tall, impressive man. 'When will you be free? There is a great deal to discuss.'

'Miss Clement, you may have the rest of the day off,' the elderly solicitor said wearily. 'Miss Winter can deal with your work. Mr. Fairgarth is only in Town for the day and I expect he has other calls on his time.'

'That's very good of you, sir—thanks.' He turned to Vanessa. 'Get your things . . . I'll wait in the car. It's a cream-coloured Jaguar parked just outside the door.' He held out his hand to the solicitor. 'Thank you for giving me so much of your time . . . if you'd care to send in your bill? I'll take over from this point.' He strode purposefully from the room.

'I don't understand . . .' Vanessa began helplessly.

Mr. Hardy smiled encouragingly. 'Sir Wilfrid Fairgarth was a very wealthy landowner. He died at the beginning of the year. It has been very difficult to trace his surviving relatives—your mother who was his sister and yourself and your sister. We only knew that his sister had married Ulric Clement and was last known to be living in a London suburb. Having discovered that she was also deceased we then had to find her child or children—and they were unknown at the last address we had.'

'I think there must be some mistake . . . my mother never spoke of having a brother.'

'I gather that she made an unsatisfactory marriage and severed all connection with her family. Once your relationship to Sir Wilfrid is established, it seems that you and your sister will no longer need to work for a living.' His smile had none of its usual frostiness . . . if by some strange quirk of fate it should prove that his secretary was also the niece and probable heiress of the wealthy Sir Wilfrid it was expedient to display warmth and friendliness now with an eye to the future when she might choose to allow Hardy and Bamber to handle her affairs. 'I advise you not to keep Mr. Fairgarth waiting—he doesn't seem a particularly patient man. And as you will probably have a great many things to deal with, it might be as well if you don't return to the office until Monday.'

'Thank you, Mr. Hardy—but I shall be in tomorrow morning,' she assured him firmly. 'Mr. Fairgarth—is he Sir Wilfrid's son?'

'Nephew, apparently, my dear—but I do believe that there is no actual blood tie. I gained the impression that he was an adopted child—but I may be wrong, of course. I expect you will shortly be conversant with all the branches of your family tree,' he added and she smiled dutifully as he expected her to do.

She hurried back to her own office in a daze. Mr. Hardy's words and manner both implied that he fully expected her to become a wealthy and useful young woman. It was so incredible that she felt sure the alarm would break through this fantastic dream at any moment.

She had never known that her mother had a brother. She had never heard of Sir Wilfrid but obviously Mr. Hardy was impressed by this sudden, amazing, newly-apparent kinship she could claim with him. Her uncle? No, it was not possible! If it were true, why had he never bothered to find them while he lived? Why had he ignored his sister's existence and allowed her to struggle with financial problems all her married life? Why had he not known her address, her circumstances and the fact of her five children?

And the haughty, arrogant, easily-disliked young man . . . was he really a cousin and why had he swept her with such hostile eyes? Had he hoped to be Sir Wilfrid's heir and now resented the existence of a cousin who might supplant him?

So many questions—and Vanessa could not yet answer any of them. She felt as though her small, comfortable world had been abruptly turned upside down and much as she had lately longed for wealth and all its attendants, now she found herself hoping that it might all be a mistake, dreading the changes that must affect their lives if she and her sisters were really the heirs to a vast fortune.

Maureen looked at her curiously. 'Whatever's the matter? You look as though you've seen a ghost! The old boy hasn't kicked the bucket, has he?' She giggled.

'No . . . something's cropped up and he's given me permission to leave now,' she replied absently, much too absorbed in her thoughts to heed Maureen's surprised and eager questions.

Deliberately, she took her time . . . tidying her desk, covering her typewriter, explaining one or two details about the work she was passing over to Maureen, running a comb through her curls and powdering her nose.

The detestable Mr. Fairgarth, cousin or not, could fume with impatience for all she cared . . . he seemed the type to expect everyone to run at his bidding and it would be as well for him to understand from the very beginning that she had a mind of her own!

The long, sleek Jaguar was waiting . . . and as she crossed the pavement, Justin Fairgarth leaned forward to open the car door. To her disappointment, he did not mention the fact that she had kept him waiting almost twenty minutes. He turned on the ignition and concentrated on manoeuvring the car into the stream of traffic.

'Where are we going?' Vanessa asked, a little shyly.

He glanced at his watch. 'It's too early for lunch—care for some coffee?'

She agreed and within a few minutes he parked the car in a side-street, helped her out and urged her swiftly along the pavement with a firm hand at her elbow. Vanessa could have wished that he was a little less forceful as she hurried on high heels by his side. At the same time, she was conscious of a reluctant admiration for his air of purpose, of knowing what he wanted and where he was going.

She stole a cautious glance at him, noting the arrogant jut of his chin, the uncompromising line of the firm yet faintly sensual mouth, the piercing blue eyes, deep-set and commanding, the hard, high cheekbones and the straight, slender nose with its ruthless flare at the nostrils. His dark, thick hair grew low on the nape of his neck and threatened to cluster in small, curling tendrils about his temples. Judging by appearances and the little she knew about him, Vanessa summed him up as a hard, impatient, tyrannical, inconsiderate, self-centred, aggressive young man who would not tolerate opposition or sentimentality.

She was rather pleased with this assessment and did not feel the slightest prick of conscience that she had attributed to him all the things she most disliked in a man. So far, she told herself firmly, he had not given her any cause to like him at all. His very hostility had incurred a swift antagonism on her part.

Justin did not miss that swift, assessing glance and he was faintly amused. She had probably made up her mind about him already and was fully prepared to dislike him—a thought that did not cause him any misgivings. He had already dismissed her as a sentimental dreamer with her eye on the main chance, a grasping, mercenary, ambitious little gold-digger who lacked the strength of mind and the necessary ruthlessness to follow through no matter how good an opening she might be granted. He had been unmoved by the childish defiance which had kept him cooling his heels outside the office for as long as she dared. He sensed that his manner had antagonised her but he had not the slightest desire to be on friendly terms with Miss Vanessa Clement or her sister.

Justin could not help thinking that life had dealt him an underhand and bitter blow by removing Sir Wilfrid from this earthly scene before he could ensure that the estate and all that went with it passed to his nephew by adoption. Superstitious to a degree, Sir Wilfrid had postponed signing his will again and again, insisting that he might be signing his own death warrant, protesting that there was time and to spare and that he had no intention of dying for many years to come. Fate had laughed in his face and he had suffered a severe stroke that was followed by a second and fatal stroke within a matter of days.

Because he had died intestate, Justin had no claim whatsoever to any part or parcel of the land or Sir Wilfrid's wealth. A bitter pill for the young man who had been brought up as the older man's son since infancy and thought of Fairlands as his natural heritage, who had devoted his love, his time and his energies to the management of the estate for the past fifteen years, who had always been assured that everything would be his in time to come.

Now, he thought bitterly, everything belonged to two complete strangers—a couple of young, foolish, ignorant girls who would not want to be bothered with Fairlands and all that it represented . . .

CHAPTER FOUR

Vanessa felt shy and confused as she faced Justin Fairgarth across the small table. She wondered if this was merely an inexplicable dream which would shatter with the strident alarum of the clock. Involuntarily she pinched herself beneath the table—but she was awake and this arrogant stranger was certainly real enough. He seemed in no hurry to explain matters as he brought out his cigarette case and opened it. Vanessa refused the offer and watched impatiently while he deliberately selected one from the case, hunted in his pockets for a lighter and finally drew deeply on the lighted cigarette.

He sat back and looked at her thoughtfully. 'You certainly resemble your mother,' he said unexpectedly.

Her eyes widened. 'You knew my mother?'

'I know the portrait of her that hangs in the Gallery at Fairlands,' he returned evenly.

'Yet you doubted my identity,' she pointed out swiftly.

'Perhaps I was reluctant to admit the likeness,' he said smoothly. 'Anyway, that office was so gloomy that it was difficult to see you properly. And you must remember that I wasn't expecting to find a Clement on the premises.'

'It was a strange coincidence,' she agreed.

'It's about time Hardy was pensioned off, in my opinion. Clement is not a common name and if it had occurred to him that you might have some connection with the Clements I wanted to find, a great deal of time could have been saved.' He spooned sugar into his coffee and stirred it thoughtfully. 'Your sister—was she too busy to follow up Hardy's letter for herself or is she so indifferent to money?'

'How could she possibly know what money was involved—any more than I did? Mr. Hardy's letter was a complete mystery to us both—but as I worked for him it seemed simple enough for me to find out what it was all about. Frankly, I didn't expect him to tell me anything—he's a stickler for doing things the correct way. But as you were there and discussing the matter—well, I couldn't keep silent, could I?'

'Of course not. You did the right thing as far as I'm concerned,' he assured her. He glanced at her curiously. She was very calm, very composed—no casual observer would suspect that a fortune had just dropped into her lap.

He did not know what an effort it was for Vanessa to conceal the shocked dismay and turbulent feelings that Mr. Hardy's revelations had evoked. She clung to the hope that it might all be a mistake—and then chided herself for being selfish. Although she might prefer to remain as she was, her sisters would undoubtedly be excited and thrilled and spend many happy hours planning their futures, knowing that their long-cherished dreams might well know fulfilment in this unexpected way.

'You seem remarkably unmoved by the thought of being wealthy,' he said drily. 'But perhaps you've always known that you and your sister were Sir Wilfrid Fairgarth's heirs.'

Anger touched her eyes. 'I've already told you that I never knew of the man's existence,' she said tartly.

'I find it difficult to believe,' he retorted. 'He was your mother's brother, after all . . . she must have spoken of her family at some time!'

'Never! We assumed that she had no family—it was something that we never really thought about,' Vanessa insisted coldly.

He gave a slight shrug. 'Odd . . .'

'Do you doubt my word?'

'Does it really matter? The important thing is that you and your sister inherit the entire Fairgarth fortune—whether or not you had any expectation of doing so.'

Vanessa caught her breath. 'I can't believe it!'

'It's really quite straightforward. Sir Wilfrid was a landowner and a very wealthy man: as the eldest son, he inherited the title, Fairlands and a tidy income from his father; your mother was his only sister, a brother drowned while on a yachting trip and the other brother, my father, died while I was still a child. I must point out that I was an adopted child—I'm not a Fairgarth by birth. Sir Wilfrid died without leaving a will and the law has it that the estate must pass to the nearest blood kin. You and your sister, being the children of his only sister Eleanor, therefore inherit everything—except the title, of course, which died with Wilfrid. Do I make myself clear, Miss Clement?'

She was very pale. 'What about you? Don't you get anything?'

'Not a penny. Does that relieve your mind?'

She ignored the sneer. 'But if we weren't interested in the estate, you would get it, surely?'

A faint, sardonic smile lurked about his mouth. 'Not interested, Miss Clement? What a fantastic theory! Well, for the sake of argument, if you and your sister were not interested there is still nothing you could do about it. You are the heirs.'

'We could sign it over to you, surely?' she insisted.

He raised an eyebrow. 'Are you in your

right mind? I can't imagine that you would want to do such a thing—and even if you did, your sister isn't likely to agree, is she?'

Vanessa shook her head, almost ruefully. 'No, no, of course not. She would think I was mad if I suggested it, too.'

'Why should you think that I'm interested in the estate, anyway?'

'You must know more about the place than we do,' she pointed out.

'Naturally . . . it's been my home since I was eight months old,' he returned smoothly.

She looked at him quickly. So her surmise had been right. He had expected to inherit everything and he was bitter and resentful at the way things had turned out. She could scarcely blame him if he had been virtually brought up by Sir Wilfrid and encouraged to believe that he was the heir, as seemed likely.

'Then you must have been like a son to Sir Wilfrid,' she said quietly. 'In which case, it seems very strange that he didn't leave a will.'

He shrugged. 'He was somewhat eccentric—didn't like the thought of wills and their implications.'

'But surely he must have known that you wouldn't get anything?'

'He didn't expect to die so soon,' he said evenly.

'Oh . . . it was very sudden?'

'A fatal stroke—or cerebral haemorrhage, if you prefer the terms of the death certificate.'

There was no hint of the very real grief he had felt at the death of the man who had been more than a father to him—and Vanessa was slightly chilled by the callous coldness of his tone.

'I still think you are entitled to everything,' she said firmly. 'After all, if Sir Wilfrid brought you up as his own son . . .'

'The law isn't interested in philanthropy of that nature,' he interrupted. 'It concerns itself only with wills and legal heirs.' He stubbed his cigarette. 'Don't cast me for the role of pauper,' he added ironically. 'I have an income of my own.'

She was so obviously relieved that he was glad that he had not enlarged on that income—four hundred a year bequeathed to him by his adoptive mother. Four hundred a year, he thought wryly, and this girl and her sister are now worth approximately forty thousand a year! Damn it, the money meant nothing—but Fairlands, how could he lose Fairlands without a protest, how could he bear to accept its inevitable sale to someone who would never love and care for the place as he had done for so long. For it was obvious that the Clements would sell the big house and its surrounding acres—city girls, office girls, what would they know or want of such magnificence, such beauty, the fine, proud heritage which should be his by right of love if not of law!

50

'I can't help feeling that we have no right to any of it,' she said uncertainly. 'If I was the sole heir, I wouldn't hesitate to sign everything over to you.'

He did not believe her. She was merely mouthing conventional platitudes because she thought that he expected them. He was contemptuous of her sentiment, such weak and easy sentiment, so much trivial concern for a complete stranger. How could he believe her to be sincere? Had it seemed to her that he was seeking her compassion, her generosity? He tried to recall what he had said and writhed inwardly at the thought that he might have betrayed his deep sense of injustice, his bitterness and his sense of loss.

'I am temporarily keeping an eye on Fairlands and the estate,' he said curtly. 'Naturally, I shall be only too pleased to hand over the responsibility to someone else—it's really too much for me to handle.' The lies came easily for he had no intention of revealing his personal feelings in the matter.

'Fairlands . . . it's a house?' Vanessa asked eagerly. Was it possible that her own dream might come true—a house in the country, a real home for herself and her sisters?

'Sorry . . . yes, of course. I'd forgotten that you know nothing of the place. It's a big house, home of the Fairgarths for several generations. It stands in its own grounds on a hill overlooking the village. Quite a pleasant

51

place. Not much good to you, I imagine . . . I suppose you will sell?'

Vanessa spread her hands in an involuntary gesture of helplessness. 'How can I say? That would depend on the others and what they want to do. If it isn't too big, too expensive to run, we might decide to live there . . . I've always wanted to live in the country,' she added shyly.

'I doubt if the expense will trouble you,' he began with deep irony and then he broke off and glanced at her with raised brows. 'Others? I thought it was only you and your sister Fiona . . . I didn't even know of *your* existence! Sir Wilfrid received a letter from your mother when Fiona was born—and that was the last news he ever had.'

Vanessa coloured slightly. 'I should have explained,' she said hastily. 'I have four sisters.'

'Good lord!' The exclamation was wrenched from him. He laughed softly. 'And half a dozen brothers, too?'

She shook her head. 'No brothers,' she said in all seriousness.

'Why on earth didn't you say so before?' he demanded.

'The opportunity didn't really arise—and I didn't think it was important.' She leaned forward. 'Is it a lot of money?' she asked impulsively, her eyes shining at the thought that her sisters might be able to follow their individual stars and not waste their time and talents in dead-end jobs.

'In the region of six thousand a year,' he replied carelessly, assuming that she referred to her own share of the income.

'Six thousand . . .' Her face brightened. A thousand a year each . . . enough to pay for Melissa's music, enough to send Rowena to a good art school, enough to support Belinda comfortably while she struggled to make a name for herself as an actress—and perhaps if she gave Fiona her share, it might be enough to start her off in a business of her own. She did not need money for anything—all she wanted was a nice little house and the company of her sisters and it might be just possible for them to run Fairlands, big though it might be, if they all contributed towards the expenses. She would not mind the work of a big house—and perhaps she could give up her job with Hardy and Bamber. Then she could devote all her time and energies to running a home for her sisters.

Her eyes were sparkling and Justin studied her curiously. What plans was she making for the spending of that six thousand? What dreams were visibly coming to life behind those grey eyes? He was slightly shaken by the incredulous, joyful delight that she unashamedly betrayed—were they then so poor, these Clements, this long-ignored, long-unknown branch of the Fairgarth family. Certainly Ulric Clement had been a struggling artist when Eleanor Fairgarth ran off with him in defiance of her family's wishes and there had never been any indication that he had made his mark in the art world. Five daughters to rear might have proved a costly business—yes, it was quite likely that money had been very short in Vanessa Clement's experience.

He assessed her appearance: neat, cheap suit of unremarkable cut and style, mock-leather bag and shoes, thin nylon gloves, hair obviously dressed at home and very little make-up. But she was an attractive young woman and her introspective silence afforded him the opportunity to imagine how she would look if she were dressed in the height of expensive fashion.

'I had no idea it would be so much,' she breathed at last.

'If your parents had been less prolific it would have been a great deal more,' he told her curtly.

'More?' She was bewildered.

'Twenty thousand instead of six if you only had to share it with your sister Fiona,' he enlarged.

Her eyes were suddenly dark with shock—dark and luminous in the ashen oval of her face. Even her lips seemed bloodless and her hands trembled so much that the coffee cup slipped from her fingers and spilled its contents across the table and into her lap.

'Are you all right?' he demanded urgently, taking a handkerchief from his breast pocket and thrusting it into her hand. He did not understand the sudden reaction—but it seemed more natural, more to be expected than her calm, easy quietness which had irritated him so much.

Automatically she scrubbed at her skirt with his spotless handkerchief while he called a waitress to wipe the table and remove the empty cups. Her mind was blank but for the echoing of the words 'twenty thousand'—and yet she still could not believe that she had heard him correctly.

He ordered fresh coffee and brought out his cigarette case. Vanessa accepted the offer this time and bent her head over the flame of his lighter. He steadied her shaking hand with his own strong, slender fingers and she thanked him with a slight, difficult smile.

'All right?' he asked again.

She nodded. 'Yes . . . but your handkerchief is ruined, I'm afraid.' She indicated the stained, sodden, crumpled linen.

'Never mind,' he said carelessly. 'You can well afford to replace it.'

Vanessa gave a strained laugh. 'Yes, I can—unless this is just a weird sort of dream and it's quite time I woke up!'

'Why should you want to wake up? Isn't it the kind of dream we'd all like to have?'

'I don't know . . . it seems to be turning into some kind of nightmare,' she said honestly. He raised a cynical eyebrow and she hurried to explain: 'It's such a lot of money . . . too much. It will make too much difference—I'm afraid . . .' Her words trailed off—impossible to explain her sudden fears and anxieties to this cold, hostile, openly incredulous stranger.

'It isn't so much between five people,' he pointed out drily.

'You really mean that we shall have six thousand pounds *each*?' she asked anxiously.

'Yes . . . I thought you realised that.'

'I thought that was the total amount.'

He smiled grimly. 'Surely you didn't think that an estate like Fairlands could be maintained on six thousand a year?'

'What do I know of Fairlands?' she retorted, recovering herself a little in face of his open contempt of her ignorance. How stupid she must seem to him—he had never known lack of money or anxiety about the future! 'Six thousand pounds seems a vast sum to me,' she went on bluntly, for it was not in her nature to dissemble, to pretend that she was not overwhelmed by the revelations of the day. 'At the moment, I'm earning just under six *hundred* pounds a year—and I consider that to be an excellent salary. To have ten times that amount for doing nothing . . . it really seems incredible to me!'

He nodded. She was still pale, still shaken. 'I'll drive you home,' he said and it was not a suggestion. 'Finish your coffee and let's be on our way.'

Vanessa was taken aback by the abruptness of his words. Evidently, as far as he was concerned, he had told her all that he considered necessary—and he would be glad to escape from her company. Her ignorance, her naivety, her shyness and lack of sophistication evidently bored and irritated him. She was not the type of woman that he had always known. He was embarrassed by her evident excitement at the news . . . he might be able to understand it but he had no wish to endure much more of her company at such a time. That was perfectly natural and she did not blame him for wanting to escape. For her part, she would be grateful for solitude, for the chance to marshal her thoughts and emotions. For the time to think about this unexpected, almost unwelcome fortune which had come their way . . .

'I can get a train quite easily,' she told him quietly. 'I've taken up too much of your time already.'

Justin did not argue. He waited until her cup was empty and her cigarette stubbed in

57

the ashtray. Then he rose to his feet and escorted her from the restaurant and along to his car with that firm hand once more beneath her elbow. He successfully conveyed the impression that it was beneath his dignity to argue the point or even to comment on her childish reluctance to allow him to drive her home.

Vanessa told him the address at his request without further protest. She did not really feel that she could cope with the train and bus journey when she had so much on her mind. Among other things was an odd sense of guilt and she stole a glance at her companion's profile as he drove, his strong hands resting lightly and capably on the steering wheel. The injustice of his position smote her very strongly. Although he might not be of Fairgarth blood, he was a member of the family to all intents and purposes and Vanessa could not help thinking that she and her sisters were usurpers. It was not surprising that there was so much hostility in his attitude. She was conscious of a great compassion for the man by her side and, despite his disclaimers, she was convinced that he had been deeply hurt and loathed the knowledge that everything he held dear would soon pass into the hands of strangers.

For they were strangers. He might be some kind of a cousin. He might know more about her mother's family than she could ever hope to know now. He might have more right to the Fairgarth money and lands, legal rights apart. But the fact remained that they were complete strangers to each other—and, glancing again at that grim profile, Vanessa was very sure that he wished them to stay that way.

She stifled a sigh. Why should it matter that he so blatantly disliked and resented her and held her in such open contempt? She wished it were possible to dislike him but her original antagonism towards this man had died and she was only conscious of compassion and interest in this difficult, arrogant stranger. She could not help thinking that he had entered her life to stay. It was unlikely that he would fade out of the picture once the legalities had been completed. If Fairlands had been his home for many years, he would have a natural interest in its treatment at strange hands and would obviously find it difficult to stay away from a place he must love. Perhaps in time the hostility would be forgotten . . . perhaps they might even call him a friend one day. Certainly the possession of wealth would bring many problems and they might be glad of his advice and assistance.

She abruptly checked her thoughts. It would be ridiculous to even think of keeping Fairlands. Impossible for them to run a big house, to manage a big estate! The only answer was to sell . . . and perhaps he was hoping for such a decision. He had claimed a private income and it was more than likely that he intended to make them feel so unwelcome, so unwanted, that they would be only too glad to sell the estate to him! It was certainly one explanation of his hostility—for there had been time in plenty for him to reconcile himself to the knowledge that strangers were to inherit the entire fortune of Sir Wilfrid Fairgarth!

CHAPTER FIVE

The traffic was heavy and it took some time to get across the river to the south side of London. But the many delays and irritating traffic tangles did not seem to bother the man by her side. She had not made any attempt at conversation and he was equally silent, concentrating on his driving.

But as soon as the roads were clearer and they were well into the suburbs, he turned his head to glance at her briefly and said: 'Tell me about your sisters. Fiona is the eldest, I presume?'

'Yes, she's twenty-five. I'm two years younger: Rowena is nearly twenty-one, Melissa is nineteen and the baby, Belinda, is eighteen.'

'Not such a baby,' he commented drily.

Vanessa smiled. 'No, not really. Fiona calls her the infant when she's in a good mood . . . the spoiled brat when Belinda does something to annoy her. I'm afraid we all spoil her most of the time.'

'Does she work?'

'She's an actress,' she returned with more than a little pride in her voice. Then she added honestly: 'Of sorts, anyway. She has a job with a small repertory company—it doesn't pay very much and she hasn't thought much of her parts so far but it's marvellous experience for her. She's very ambitious, of course . . .'

'Her name in lights, eh?'

She fancied that he sneered and the swift colour rushed to her cheeks. 'That's perfectly natural, isn't it?' she defended. 'She's quite good . . . I don't see why she shouldn't make a name for herself one day. I only wish we could have afforded to send her to RADA.'

'You can now,' he reminded her carelessly.

'Oh . . . yes, I suppose so.' She still could not accept the fact of their newfound wealth.

'And the others?' he prompted as she sat silent for a few minutes, thinking of Belinda and her transports of delight when she learned the news. 'Are they equally ambitious?'

'We're quite a talented family, as it happens. Rowena paints and she's sold a few

61

pictures already. Fiona is artistic too but dress designing is her interest. Melissa is musical—she's always wanted to be a concert pianist.'

'Quite an assortment of talents,' he commented.

'My father was a very talented man,' she said swiftly. 'Fiona and Rowena have inherited his gift. My mother was very musical—that explains Melissa. I don't know where the dramatic ability came from—but then I've never known very much about my family background on either side.'

'What about you?' he asked idly. 'It only remains for you to admit that you are a writer in your spare time—and then all the talents are covered.'

She resented his sardonic tone. 'I have no particular talent for anything,' she said coldly. 'It takes all my time looking after the girls and working in an office.'

His mouth twitched with amusement. 'What happened—no fairies at your christening?'

'There has to be a practical person in every family,' she retorted.

'And you are practical?' He could not help the faint incredulity behind the words for he had assessed her as a dreamer who preferred the world of fantasy to that of reality.

'I have to be,' she said tartly. 'You've no idea what it's like living with four sisters who invariably have their heads in the clouds—someone has to have their feet firmly on the ground if only to deal with the cooking and the washing-up and the shopping and cleaning and bed-making . . .'

'Not to mention the washing and the ironing,' he supplied as she ran out of breath.

'That too,' she told him crisply.

'I imagine you must be quite indispensable.'

She bit her lip involuntarily. How horrible of him to sneer! Perhaps she had sounded rather fussy and old-maidish and prim . . . but she had only told the truth. Not for the first time, she cursed the tongue that was too free at times.

'Someone has to do it,' she repeated defensively.

'Hard luck that you happen to be that someone,' he said quietly.

She stiffened. She did not want his sympathy either. She did all those things for her sisters because she wanted to do them, because she enjoyed doing them—and she had not told him about them to cast herself in the rôle of Cinderella. 'I don't think so.'

He threw her a fleeting glance. 'You'll have to direct me from this point,' he merely said.

Vanessa was glad to change the subject . . . and thankful that the journey was nearly at an end. 'It isn't very far now . . . take the first turning on your right beyond the traffic lights and then the third on your left,' she said.

He slowed the car as they turned into the quiet, shabby street and glanced at the house numbers. Within a few seconds, he pulled into the kerb outside the big house.

Vanessa hunted in her bag for the key as he stepped out to the pavement and walked around the car to open the door for her. He helped her out and followed her to the stone steps that led up to the front door.

She hesitated and looked up at him. 'Thank you—it was kind of you to come so far out of your way. I hope you haven't had to change any of your plans.'

'They were not important.' He stepped back to study the big house.

Vanessa was at a loss. He did not seem impatient to get away . . . she did not know whether to invite him in or not. It was almost one o'clock and she was beginning to feel hungry . . .

'Fiona will be home soon,' she said uncertainly. 'It's Thursday—early closing day for the dress shop where she works. Would you care to come in and wait for her—after all, she was the one you really wanted to talk to about the estate.'

He glanced at his own watch. 'I think I should see your sister,' he agreed. 'Is there a decent restaurant in this locality—somewhere we can have lunch and then come back here?'

'If you'll trust my cooking, I can rustle up

some food for us both,' she said lightly.

He looked down at her with a faint smile. 'If your sisters don't complain about your cooking, why should I?'

That smile, faint though it was, cheered her unexpectedly. Perhaps he was really quite a nice person—if one could only penetrate that barrier of hostility and indifference!

She laughed easily. 'Oh, they do complain—but they survive. I'm no *cordon bleu* but I do my best.' She opened the door and entered the house. Justin went to lock the car doors and then joined her in the hall.

As they mounted the narrow stairs, Vanessa hoped that the flat would be as neat as she had left it that morning. Belinda had still been in bed when she left, having no morning rehearsal that day and within half an hour Belinda could turn the tidiest of rooms upside down. She had only just remembered that Belinda might be home and she turned to warn her companion. Her unexpected hesitation took him by surprise and his hand moved swiftly to steady her. Colour stormed into her face at his nearness . . . one step below her, they were now of equal height and she found herself looking directly into those piercing blue eyes.

'Belinda isn't at the theatre today . . .' The words trailed off.

His eyes were an amazingly deep blue, fringed by thick black lashes, and because she had startled him, they had lost the already-familiar coldness and arrogance of expression. They seemed warm and human and oddly attractive—and Vanessa was furious with her heart for skipping a beat.

She recovered herself. 'I expect Belinda is home—so be prepared to find the place looking as though a hurricane has just swept through it. She is the untidiest girl!'

He nodded. 'You don't need to impress me,' he returned drily—and his eyes were cold steel once again and Vanessa was conscious once more of a faint chill in the region of her heart. He was so determined to be unfriendly—and sudden depression stole over her again.

She went on and led the way into the living-room. Her fears had been fully justified and she knew a swift tide of annoyance. Magazines and scripts littered the floor: an ashtray had been knocked from the table and scattered its contents over the carpet; an empty cup in its slop-filled saucer was perched on an arm of the settee and flimsy articles of underclothing were generally scattered about the room. She turned to him with an apology hovering on her lips and found him surveying the room with obvious amusement.

'I see what you mean,' he murmured.

Without making the apology, Vanessa began to pick up the magazines and the

66

scripts. Justin scooped up an armful of clothing and looked about him for somewhere to put it.

At that moment, Belinda came in, rubbing her long, wet hair in a thick towel. 'You're early, Fiona,' she said carelessly. 'I was in the bath when I heard you coming up.' Another thick towel was wrapped about her slim body and tucked casually into its folds . . . long, bare legs still sparkled with water, the firm, youthful curve of her breasts was barely covered by the towel which threatened to come adrift at any moment.

Horrified, Vanessa stared at her, speechless.

Considerately, Justin turned away but not before he had absorbed and appreciated the beauty of that slender youthfulness.

'Belinda!' Vanessa found her voice at last.

Her sister tossed back the thick mane of her hair, startled by the shocked dismay and embarrassment in Vanessa's voice. 'What on earth . . . ?' Then she saw the tall, unknown man. 'Oh . . . ! She fled from the room.

Vanessa could scarcely meet his eyes. 'I'm sorry—she's such a scatterbrain . . .'

'She has every right to wander about clad only in a towel in her own home,' he said easily. 'And she didn't expect you to be home with a strange man in tow.' He added with a smile: 'She's remarkably pretty.'

Vanessa abruptly realised his burden. 'Oh,

let me take those things,' she said hastily. He surrendered them readily and she moved towards the door. 'Would you excuse me for a moment . . . I'll have a look in the fridge and find out what I can offer you.'

The door closed behind her and Justin wandered about the room, studying the paintings that hung on the walls, the books on the shelves, the canvas that stood on an easel by the window. It was a pleasant and comfortable room, a homely room—and by all accounts, it was Vanessa Clement's efforts that made it so.

She puzzled him. She was much more difficult to assess than he had thought at first. One moment she seemed warm and friendly and appealing: the next moment, she was snapping a cold, biting retort and withdrawing behind those lovely grey eyes. One moment she seemed youthful, naive in her natural candour, openly friendly and at ease: the next moment, she was mature, poised, aloof, watching her words carefully, shyness hovering behind the veneer of self-assurance.

He smiled to himself. How shocked she had been by her sister's unconventional garb! But how perfectly natural for a girl to wander in and out of rooms in her own home when she believed that only a sister was about, wrapped only in a towel. She had explained that she was taking a bath—and she had evidently washed her hair. No one could have expected the girl to dress before greeting her sister!

He had been neither shocked nor embarrassed. But he had known a swift sympathy for Vanessa's dismay. For his part, Belinda could have walked in wearing only the beautiful, pearly skin that nature had given her and he would have remained completely unmoved. But he appreciated that Vanessa could not know that—and he hoped she was not scolding her sister too harshly at that very moment.

Belinda turned on her sister as she entered the bedroom. 'You might have warned me!' she said furiously. 'I've never felt such a fool in all my life!'

'How was I to know you were in the bath—or that you'd come bursting in like that?' Vanessa retorted in justified indignation. 'You are an idiot, Belinda! Even if it had been Fiona you know perfectly well that she often has a man with her when she's only come in to change before going out for the afternoon. I've told you a dozen times not to wander about half-naked!'

Belinda pulled a dress over her head. 'What are you doing home anyway? It's only one o'clock,' she said sulkily.

'I know the time as well as you do! When you're dressed, I'll explain.' Crossly, Vanessa walked out of the room and closed the door with a sharp little snap.

Justin came out of the living-room as she mounted the three little steps that divided the sleeping quarters from the living quarters.

'Can I help?'

'Oh . . . no, thanks.' She caught at the ravelled threads of her temper and managed to smile at him. 'Could you bear my interpretation of spaghetti bolognese?'

'I could be polite about it, anyway,' he drawled, amusement tugging at his mouth.

She laughed, appreciating the rare moment of friendliness. 'That's all I ask—believe me, you don't know how rude sisters can be to each other at times.' She opened the kitchen door. 'I'll be with you in a minute, Mr. Fairgarth.'

He accepted his dismissal and returned to the living-room. He sat down in one of the deep armchairs, brought out his cigarettes and prepared to wait. He did not have to wait long before the door was opened slightly, a dark head looked into the room, a slight gasp was heard and the door closed again abruptly. The walls were thin and he could hear the sound of voices coming from the next room.

Then Vanessa came in with a tray. 'I don't know how you feel about more coffee,' she said uncertainly. 'I thought I'd make it now—it won't seem so long before lunch is ready then.'

'An excellent idea,' he approved carelessly.

70

He jerked his head in the direction of the door. 'Is she shy about facing me again?'

She hesitated a moment, then she said in a low voice: 'I've just told her that she'll never make an actress if she can't walk into this room as though nothing had happened. She's probably working on her lines . . . a natural indignation has overcome any feeling of embarrassment.' Her eyes twinkled at him as though they were conspirators.

Even as she spoke, Belinda sailed into the room, the thick mass of her hair piled high on her head, her mouth gleaming with swift application of lipstick, her hands outstretched towards Justin as though she greeted a dear, long-absent friend.

'How nice! I do hope I haven't kept you waiting too long—but I know you will overlook my tardy arrival. You must remember that punctuality was never one of my strong points, my dear.' The sophisticated drawl, the arch smile, the eager approach almost convulsed Justin—but he manfully controlled his instinct to laugh, leaped to his feet, took her slim hands in his own and bowed courteously over them.

'The moments of eager anticipation, long though they seemed, are forgotten now that we are together again, my love,' he murmured softly, caressingly.

Startled, Belinda snatched away her hands and threw him a reproachful glance. Then her sense of humour triumphed and she laughed. 'Very good on the spur of the moment. Benjamin would adore you! I suppose you're not looking for a job.'

'Not at the moment,' he agreed smoothly.

Vanessa occupied herself with the coffee cups, wondering at the strange desolation which overwhelmed her as they laughed together like old friends. He had evidently captivated Belinda's liking with the minimum of effort—and it was equally obvious that he was prepared to like Belinda on sight. How pointed his manner in comparison with the cold hostility she had experienced ever since they had met! Then she checked the odd jealousy, angry with herself. He had adroitly forestalled any embarrassment that Belinda might have felt and his swift sizing-up of Belinda's dramatic entrance and immediate reaction, so very right, demanded her respect and admiration. What did it matter if they liked each other, if they could laugh together? They might see a great deal of him in the future and it would be nice for Belinda to feel that he was a friend. And Belinda's easy manner and youthful gaiety might succeed in breaking down the hostility he obviously felt towards the Clements—and that would be an excellent thing.

Belinda accepted her coffee cup from Vanessa and threw her a mute glance of reminder. Despite her pleadings, she was still completely in the dark as to the identity of this stranger and could only assume that he was a friend that Vanessa had never mentioned before.

'Oh . . . Belinda, this is Mr. Fairgarth—a cousin of sorts,' she supplied dutifully.

Belinda's eyes widened. 'A cousin?'

'Justin Fairgarth,' he amended. His tone, directed at Vanessa, indicated openly that she might have been interested enough to have asked his first name before this moment arose.

'What a lovely name!' Belinda exclaimed. 'It would be perfect if you did join the Benjamin Rep. Is it your real name—or are you an actor, after all?'

'Belinda!' Vanessa's low voice held a warning.

Justin smiled. 'No, I'm not an actor—and the name seems ordinary enough to me.'

'But it's so dramatic! Justin Fairgarth—I think it's delightful! Justin . . . it suits you enormously, you know. It's a dark name, you see.' Her lower lip pouted prettily for a moment. 'Belinda is a fair name—so annoying. I wanted to call myself Rosalind Clement but Benjamin wouldn't hear of it.'

'Rosalind being a dark name, of course,' he said in perfect understanding.

Vanessa sighed. She rose and slipped from the room, certain that they would not notice her absence. As she prepared the bolognese,

73

kept an eye on the spaghetti, washed the salad and opened tins of fruit and cream, she could hear their voices in eager, lively discussion—and again she felt that unaccountable sensation of being excluded from their easy intimacy.

Justin was enjoying himself. This chit of a girl was amusing, lively and remarkably pretty even if she did have some colourful, fantastic theories. But it seemed that Vanessa was a long time from the room and he wondered how often she busied herself with domestic affairs while her sisters devoted themselves to the entertainment of guests or occupied themselves with their own interests.

The door opened and he looked up with a half-smile, expecting Vanessa. A young woman glanced into the room, murmured something he did not catch and closed the door once more. Belinda did not even turn her head, intent on her search through a reference book to prove a point that they had been arguing about. Fiona, he guessed—not difficult to surmise as she was expected and she bore a strong resemblance to Belinda. In that fleeting moment, he had been impressed by a dark, tempestuous, striking beauty— what a furore these Clements would cause when they entered society with their looks and their wealth for support . . .

CHAPTER SIX

As Justin mounted the stone steps to the massive front door of Fairlands, the sound of an approaching car gave him pause and he turned to lift a hand in friendly salute to the driver.

Morny Fitzgerald braked, turned off the ignition and smiled at him warmly. 'Just back?' she asked easily, omitting to mention that she had seen his car pass her house and immediately hurried out to follow him in the sleek white sports car.

He nodded. 'Nicely timed,' he said drily. They had known each other since childhood and were on the easiest of terms. But far from being flattered by Morny's obvious determination to add him to her long list of conquests, he found her tactics rather blatant and irritating—and found it impossible to work up any romantic tendency towards the beautiful, sophisticated Morny.

She smoothed back a tendril of her flaming auburn hair, piled high on her head. 'I'm selling tickets for the Charity Ball,' she said lightly. 'Can I persuade you to buy a dozen this year?'

'Possibly . . . I might make up a party. Come in and have a drink?'

She stepped from the car with alacrity.

'What a lovely suggestion!' She linked her hand in his arm. 'How was London?'

'Much as usual.'

'No luck?'

'I wouldn't call it luck,' he said, a trifle grimly, 'but I have found the Clements.'

She raised an eyebrow. 'In the plural?'

'Five of them.'

'Good heavens! But how typical of a struggling artist to have so many children,' she said scornfully. 'Are they impossible, darling—or haven't you seen them yet?'

'I've met them all. That's why I'm so late home—they are all working girls and I had to wait until this evening to meet them en masse.'

She wrinkled her shapely little nose. 'What a bore for you! Was it very grim?'

'Not at all. They are very attractive young women,' he said brusquely.

She glanced at him through the thick veil of her long lashes. 'But you didn't like them.'

He shrugged. 'I don't have to like them, my dear. In any case, I was rather overwhelmed—trying to impress on five temperamental women that the whole thing isn't just a practical joke is a little much for any man!'

He walked to the sideboard and began to pour the drinks. Morny watched him thoughtfully. He was really a most attractive man . . . it was most unfortunate that he was

76

now a very poor one. She had made up her mind to marry him but that was out of the question now. Love in a cottage was not her aim—and although Justin might not be quite reduced to that, he was no longer such an eligible proposition—Fairlands and its rolling acres and its attendant wealth together with Justin's good looks and personality was one thing . . . Justin with only a meagre income and no home of his own was entirely another.

'I do think the whole thing is terribly unfair, Justin,' she said warmly. 'I don't suppose these wretched girls have the slightest interest in Fairlands—and everyone knows how much it means to you.'

He gave her a drink and smiled down at her. 'It means a lot to you, doesn't it, Morny?'

She sighed. 'I love this place . . . I've always wanted it. It's hateful to think of it passing to strangers.'

'Rather unfortunate that Aunt Eleanor had five girls instead of an attractive only son, isn't it?'

Faint colour stained her cheeks. 'I don't understand you,' she said haughtily.

He smiled. 'You and I have always understood each other very well, my dear. You know perfectly well what I mean. If I'd stepped into Wilfrid's shoes you'd have been ordering your trousseau by now!'

Her eyes narrowed. She was not quite sure

how to interpret his words. Did he mean that he would not have hesitated to ask her to marry him if he now owned Fairlands and Sir Wilfrid's wealth? Or had she been too obvious in her determination to marry him until Sir Wilfrid's death had forced her to change her plans?

'Would I?' she asked slowly, playing for time.

Unexpectedly he bent his head to kiss her smooth cheek. 'Who knows? You're a very lovely woman and any man would be proud to have you for a wife,' he said lightly. 'Certainly you would have graced Fairlands in a way that is completely beyond the Clement sisters. You were made for this magnificence—they were not.'

She held his gaze for a long moment. Then she looked away, surprised by the tears that sprang swiftly to her eyes. 'Oh . . . Justin, that's a perfect compliment,' she said unsteadily, convinced now that he loved her, that he had wanted to marry her, that he had courageously put aside his hopes and dreams rather than expose her to the difficulties of marriage with a poor man! 'I . . . I only wish things had been different.'

'Our lives are mapped out for us,' he said smoothly. 'We can only be blown by the winds of chance and accept the inevitable.' He placed his hand beneath her chin and tilted her face. 'Never mind, my sweet—there are plenty of other rich men in the country.'

She wrenched away from his hand and the mockery in his eyes. 'How can you! You know that I don't care a fig for money!'

'Because you've never felt the want of it,' he said shrewdly. 'Be honest, Morny—you'd never marry a man who couldn't give you everything you've always had . . . and more besides!'

'I might,' she said hesitantly.

His mouth quirked with amusement. 'Will you marry me?'

She stared at him blankly for a second. Then she pulled herself together hastily and the undeniable truth in her eyes was swiftly concealed. 'You're not in love with me,' she said flatly.

'Are you so sure?' He caught her by the slim shoulders and challenged her to meet his eyes.

Morny laughed shakily. 'Of course I'm sure! I'm still wearing pigtails and a brace on my teeth as far as you're concerned—you've never really thought of me as a woman!'

His eyes mocked her tenderly. Then he released her shoulders and moved to pour himself another drink. 'I'm teasing you, my sweet,' he said lightly. 'You needn't lose any sleep worrying about my broken heart, you know. I'm not in love with any women—not even the beautiful and very desirable Morny Fitzgerald. And I might add that you've been a woman to me for many, many years and if I was capable of loving anyone, I would probably have fallen in love with you years ago.' He turned to smile at her. 'I'll take a dozen of those tickets, by the way—and ask you now if you'll join my party.'

She was relieved by the turn of subject—but later she would dwell on his words and wish with all her heart that he had inherited Fairlands for surely he must be one of the kindest, most generous, most warm-hearted men in the world!

'I'd love to, Justin. Who else is going with you?'

'My new-found cousins, of course—and I shall have to rustle up some men. Raif might join us, do you think?'

'I'll ask him,' she promised. She looked at Justin over the rim of her glass as she sipped her sherry. 'Do you think they'll care for the ball, Justin? If they are so ordinary won't they feel a little ill at ease?'

'They'll have to get used to such occasions, won't they? And the Ball will give them the opportunity to meet most of their new neighbours. Besides, I wouldn't say they were "ordinary", Morny . . . they have a certain percentage of Fairgarth blood and I would say that it takes precedence over the Clement. They won't disgrace Fairlands . . . if they decide to live here, that is!'

Morny sat down in a deep chair. 'Tell me
80

about them?' she invited curiously.

'That would spoil the surprise,' he returned lightly. 'I've invited—or rather suggested that they should come here for the weekend. So you will soon meet them for yourself.'

She pouted prettily. 'How will you go on with a pack of females about the place, darling? This has always been such a male stronghold.'

He grinned. 'Brighten the place up a bit. Oh, they won't bother me. Anyway, I won't be here much longer, you know. Once they take over the reins, I'm getting out.'

Her eyes widened. 'But where will you go? What will you do? They surely can't mean to turn you out—who will manage the estate?'

Justin shrugged. 'I mean to turn myself out. I haven't made up my mind about my future yet—but I shall find something. I've had an excellent training in estate management, after all.'

'Get a job, do you mean!'

Her tone was so incredulous that he laughed. 'Of course! Four hundred a year isn't going to keep me, Morny. Don't look so horrified—I'm not a stranger to work. Running Fairlands doesn't entail sitting down with my feet up and a book in my hand, you know.'

'If only Wilfrid knew what he's done to you,' she mourned.

'I expect he does,' he returned cheerfully.

'I can just see him turning to his fellow-departed and grunting: "*Do the boy good—fend for himself a little. He's always had everything too easy. I've spoiled the boy, damme if I haven't!*" It's up to me to prove that I *can* fend for myself, Morny.'

'Well, I wish you may succeed,' she said tartly.

'Your faith in me is touching,' he retorted drily.

She rose and went to him eagerly. 'Oh, I don't doubt that you'll get a job, that you'll make a success of anything you take up, Justin. But how will you live without Fairlands? What will fill that void? This place is your life—you'll be utterly lost without it! It's wicked, unfair, cruel!' Tears sparkled on her dark lashes.

She voiced his own thoughts but he would not betray the dark, painful bitterness within his heart. He smiled with an ease that belied his feelings. 'You're making too much of it all, Morny. Yes, I love this place. It will be a wrench to leave it, I admit. But perhaps it will be for the best. It isn't a good thing for any man to be obsessed by a house, by land, by pride of possession. My life? Yes, Fairlands has always been my life—but what an admission for a man of thirty-one to make! If I'd been less absorbed in Fairlands all these years I might have had what other men hold dear . . . a wife and children. There are other things in life besides Fairlands and now I have the chance to look for them.' He touched her cheek with his fingers, gently, caressingly. 'Don't be sorry for me, Morny—it isn't a tragedy.'

'It's like you to make light of it,' she said quietly. 'But I know what a blow it was to you.'

'I'm not denying that . . . but I've had time to get used to the idea and time to think about the good things that might come of it.'

'If they don't sell Fairlands they might ask you to stay on and manage the estate for them,' she suggested hopefully. 'You would do that, surely? You wouldn't be too proud?'

'I really don't know. I think it's unlikely that they'll keep Fairlands, anyway. I might stay on for a while if they wanted it that way . . . but only until they had found their feet.' He smiled. 'I'm quite fired with enthusiasm for the idea of getting away and looking at life through eyes that aren't blinded by the beauty of this place, you know. Lately I've been wondering what I'm missing by keeping my nose to the grindstone.'

'Not very much,' she said cynically. 'I've seen it all and I still prefer Fairlands.'

'Perhaps the Clements will sell it to a handsome young bachelor and you can set your snares in earnest,' he teased.

'He wouldn't be a patch on you,' she told him, almost sorrowfully.

'He'd probably make a much better husband,' he retorted easily. He walked over to the writing bureau and found his cheque book. 'Those tickets, Morny—what's the damage? I'll give you a cheque for them now, shall I?'

'It might be wiser for you to wait and see if the Clements want to go to the Ball,' she told him.

He shrugged. 'I can always find plenty of people to make up a party.'

He put the tickets safely into a pigeon-hole of the bureau and restored his cheque book to its customary place. They talked for a few more minutes and then Morny reluctantly took her leave of him. He watched her car out of sight, a look of tender indulgence in his eyes. He was really very fond of Morny and he was touched by her concern for him. But the hurt went so deep that he could not bear anyone's sympathy, anyone's concern, no matter how sincere or how well-meant. He had done his best to treat the whole thing lightly whenever the subject was mentioned by his friends and they, knowing his love for Fairlands and sensing what it meant to him to lose it, had followed his lead.

But Morny, dear, lovable Morny, lovable despite her faults or perhaps because of them, Morny either could not or would not stay clear of the subject. He admitted that it was difficult, that he could scarcely expect her not to talk about Fairlands when he had kept her well informed on the progress he was making in his search for Sir Wilfrid's only blood kin. Naturally she was interested—and naturally she was concerned . . .

Justin knew perfectly well that Morny had hoped to marry him. He also knew that with the realisation that Fairlands had not passed to him, as everyone in the vicinity had expected, she had changed her mind—and he did not blame her in the least. The only daughter of wealthy and indulgent parents whose every whim and fancy had been granted throughout her life was not likely to marry a man who had nothing but a mere pittance. It was not only that, of course, for she could expect an excellent marriage settlement from her father. Fairlands had been her goal—to be the mistress of Fairlands—and although she might be very fond of him, she would not marry him if he could not bestow that position upon her.

She was not in love with him. Justin knew that and was thankful. If Morny loved him she would disregard his lack of money, his lack of Fairlands and his lack of family background for as an adopted child he had never known anything about his real parents or their social status. He was also very thankful that he had never been in danger of loving Morny . . . for it would have been too much, to lose Fairlands and the girl he loved in one fell stroke.

He turned and went back into the house to draw up a chair to the blazing log fire with the decanter on the table by his side, an open box of cigarettes and his thoughts.

It had been an odd sort of day. Beginning with that unexpected, coincidental meeting with Vanessa Clement and ending with the hour he had spent in the company of all five of the Clement girls. It had been difficult to convince them that he was perfectly serious and that they really had inherited Fairlands and its vast wealth. Vanessa had left him to do the talking—had left him to flounder his way through, in actual fact, although he knew that she no longer doubted the truth of his story. She had sat in silence, a faint smile playing about her mouth while a strange sadness in her eyes vied with that smile—and her sisters, in varying degrees of shock, excitement, incredulity, had each tried to out-talk the others.

They were a motley collecton of young women: Vanessa, quiet, reserved, domesticated, mothering her lively ·sisters; Fiona, strikingly beautiful, wilful, very sure of herself and knowing what she wanted from life, Rowena and Melissa, like enough to be twins in looks and temperament, absorbed in their own world of dreams and hopes and ambitions, resentful of the circumstances which had so far prevented them from achieving those ambitions; and Belinda, young, impetuous, eager, mischievous and very appealing despite the tendency to act as much off-stage as on.

Justin had summed them up swiftly and he prided himself on being an excellent judge of character. He could not admit to feeling any particular liking for any of them but at the same time he was honest enough to grant that his bitterness and resentment prevented him from liking the women he thought of as intruders and usurpers. He had no reason to dislike them: he had no reason to like them. So he could think of them dispassionately and wonder how they would adjust to a completely new world and way of life.

Belinda, of course, was already visualising herself in society—a natural success, the belle of every ball, trailing a dozen admirers in her wake and skilfully avoiding the poisoned arrows from her rivals.

He felt that Rowena and Melissa would remain very much as they were now . . . indifferent to money except as it affected their choice of careers, dreamy, sensitive, introspective and completely self-centred, allowing the world to pass them by as long as Rowena had her painting and Melissa her music.

Vanessa . . . he did not need to wonder about her feelings. She had shown only too plainly that she was interested in money—and if she had been struggling to keep them all in comfort on the bare minimum of money for the last few years then her attitude was quite understandable. She could not be blamed for wanting to be free of the worry and responsibility—and no doubt she had had a surfeit of domesticity. She had probably earned her good fortune.

His thoughts turned to Fiona . . . and met a dead end. He felt that she was very much a mystery to him. She had an even greater reserve than Vanessa and she did not show her feelings at all. She was very much mistress of herself. It struck him that her manner would have been much the same if she had known of the relationship between her mother and Sir Wilfrid Fairgarth and fully expected to inherit Fairlands in due course. He did not think she had known . . . but she had betrayed no surprise or excitement—nothing in fact but a calm acceptance which was slightly antagonising. He felt that she would walk into Fairlands as though it had always been her home—and that nothing and no one would ever jar her self-possession. Rather an irritating young woman, in fact, he thought on a rising tide of resentment and wished he had not suggested that they visit Fairlands that weekend. It would have been wiser to make his own arrangements for the future and make sure he was miles away from the place he loved before their invasion . . .

CHAPTER SEVEN

The car turned in the big white gates and moved slowly along the curving drive of the beautiful old house to the accompaniment of gasps and exclamations.

'Isn't it lovely!'

'Is it really ours?'

'Pinch me, someone—I must be dreaming! I just can't believe it's true!'

'What a perfect place!'

Only Vanessa sat silent, wishing she could turn back the clock. Nothing had been the same since Thursday evening and she was dreading the future. For her sisters were already behaving as though they were the daughters of Croesus and the many contemptuous references to the way they had been living until now had shocked and hurt her deeply.

Fiona turned to her impatiently. 'Are you still sulking? Can't you find anything to say about the place?' They had agreed about the hired car which had seemed an unnecessary extravagance to Vanessa and an absolute necessity to Fiona who wanted to arrive in style. But then they had disagreed about so many things during the past thirty-six hours and Vanessa was beginning to wonder why she tried to argue with her determined sisters who were looking forward to a lazy, pampered existence as wealthy members of society.

'It's beautiful,' she said dutifully.

'But . . . ?' Fiona mocked. There had been so many 'buts' from Vanessa since Thursday.

Vanessa shrugged. 'What has it to do with us? We don't belong here, Fiona . . . we have no real right to this lovely house and these beautiful grounds.'

'Nonsense! We have more right that Justin Fairgarth, if that's what is worrying you. He isn't even a Fairgarth in fact.'

The car drew up outside the house and Fiona turned away from her sister with a gesture of scornful annoyance. Justin came out of the house and slowly descended the wide steps, trying not to play the part of host to these girls who were now the owners of Fairlands, determined not to feel that he had no right to be showing them over the place which was rightfully and legally theirs and which they should have known since childhood.

Fiona nodded to him. It was a cool, composed little nod that chilled him. Melissa and Rowena advanced slowly, almost shyly. Belinda ran forward to meet him, her pretty face alive with enjoyment of the moment.

'Are you going to do a conductd tour?'

He smiled. 'Not just now. I've ordered coffee for eleven o'clock.' He glanced at his watch. 'You made good time on the road.'

'He was a jolly good driver. I'm going to have a car of my own . . . will you teach me to drive, Justin?'

He looked down at her lively, laughing face. 'If I'm around,' he promised idly.

Fiona walked past them and into the house stripping off her gloves. Justin watched her, his eyes inscrutable. It was just as he had expected . . . she had a certain air about her, a poise and hauteur and easy self-possession, as she entered the house and she scarcely glanced about her as though she had lived there all her life and knew every detail of the beautiful, panelled hall with its glittering chandeliers and wide, graceful staircase. Belinda tugged at his arm and he walked the last few steps by her side, followed by the girls he mentally thought of as 'the twins'. Then he rememberd Vanessa and turned on the thought of her. She was standing by the car, looking so lost and lonely that his heart tugged unexpectedly. Detaching himself from Belinda with a murmured excuse, he ran down the steps.

'Won't you come in?' he asked quietly.

She nodded. 'Yes . . . in a moment.' She stayed by the car, studying the long, low, rambling house of mellow brick.

Justin followed her gaze. 'Pleasant, eh?' he

murmured with justifiable pride.

Vanessa turned to look at him. 'We don't belong here,' she said steadily.

He was taken aback. 'I hope I haven't said or done anything to make you feel like that. You and your sisters have more right to Fairlands than I have, you know.'

'Perhaps . . . in law. But you love this place . . . and to us it's just an unfamiliar house that will present many difficulties if we decide to keep it.' A faint sigh escaped her lips. 'And there seem to be enough problems without Fairlands to add to them.'

He resented her lack of enthusiasm and seeming ingratitude for the gift of a house and land that he dearly loved and had always expected to own. 'Problems?' he asked incredulously. 'Many people would welcome the problems that attach to your good fortune.'

She moved impatiently towards the steps. 'I didn't expect *you* to understand,' she said coldly. She quickened her pace at Belinda's call and Justin followed shortly, chilled and annoyed by that obvious dismissal.

It was not a good beginning and the atmosphere was decidedly tinged with hostility as they sat in the large, impressive drawing-room over coffee and cigarettes.

Fiona treated him with a cool indifference and questioned him with a shrewd pertinence about the estate, its income and expenditure and its management, which made him feel little more than a paid caretaker. Melissa and Rowena were impatient to see over the house and wanted to know how many rooms, how many servants, how many cars and horses until his head seemed to spin with their inane questions and girlish enthusiasm. Belinda's possessive airs were no longer amusing and he longed to tell her bluntly that her dramatic poses did not impress him in the least and would not go down very well with their new neighbours in the future. Vanessa scarcely smiled, replied to any remark in monosyllables and seemed to have no interest whatsoever in Fairlands.

Matters were not improved when they did the grand tour of the house and he had to listen while they discussed alterations and improvements, criticised this and approved that and squabbled over the assignment of the bedrooms.

'You've decided not to sell, then?' he asked Fiona.

She looked at him haughtily. 'Did you think we would, Mr. Fairgarth?'

'The idea crossed my mind . . . Fairlands is quite a responsibility, you know.'

'We shall manage. You'll stay on, of course—as estate manager. It will be worth your while, I promise.'

Anger turned his eyes to steel. 'I'm afraid that's out of the question.'

She shrugged. 'As you please.' But she could not quite conceal the dismay and chagrin in her eyes.

He said coldly: 'I'll stay until you've found your feet, of course. I've no intention of leaving you in the lurch. I'll look around for a reliable man to take my place, if you wish.'

'I should be most grateful.'

Her patronising tone, her *grand dame* manner had the power to set his teeth on edge and he turned away as Belinda was laying down the law about the lovely room with its wide, sweeping view of the fields that she was claiming for her own.

'Sorry,' he said brusquely. 'That happens to be my room.'

She was disconcerted but only for a moment. 'Then I'll have the one next door,' she said emphatically.

'But I must have that view,' Rowena argued. 'Don't be so pushing, Belinda . . . as the youngest, you should let us have the choice and then take what's left!'

'While you fight it out, I'll go down and help Madison with your cases,' Justin said hurriedly. 'I expect you'll want to freshen up before lunch.'

Vanessa waited until he was out of earshot and then turned on her sisters crossly. 'Do you have to behave like spoiled children? What does it matter where you sleep? Goodness knows what he must think of your manners! This isn't our house yet . . . try to remember that we are Mr. Fairgarth's guests!'

'Nonsense!' Fiona said firmly. 'This *is* our house, virtually. Mr. Fairgarth is little more than an employee of the estate.'

'And unpaid, at that!' Vanessa retorted. 'Have you no consideration for his feelings? This has always been his home . . . still is, for that matter! I'm ashamed of you all.'

'Oh, don't be so stuffy, Van,' Melissa said easily. 'We should worry what he thinks . . . soon we'll be living here in this beautiful house and it will be up to him to consider our feelings and our wishes in everything. Won't it be a lovely change to give orders instead of taking them? I'm really looking forward to being a lady of the manor!'

'He isn't staying,' Fiona said.

Vanessa stared. 'What do you mean—isn't staying?'

'I asked him to carry on with the management of the estate and he turned me down, very rudely. But he did agree to stay until he's found someone to take his place.'

Vanessa's eyes sparkled with the light of battle. 'I suppose you offered him a salary! A salary to do the job he loves, the job he's always done for nothing and been glad to do! How could you, Fiona! What necessity was there to ask him to stay? This is his home . . . he lives here and is free to live here as long as he likes, for my part. You seem to have forgotten that he's our cousin, that he's entitled to come and go as he pleases and that we should be damned grateful to have him around to run the estate. What do we know about such things? How could we run it? And what good will it do us if he goes and we have a stranger to manage the estate . . . we could be cheated right and left and never know it! What a fool you are!'

'Have you quite finished?' Fiona said icily. 'Look here, Van, we're doing him the favour by asking him to stay—we could turn him out the minute the legalities are settled with right on our side and he knows it! You can regard him as a cousin, if you like—I certainly don't. He isn't even a Fairgarth . . . and, what's more to the point, he's a stranger and could cheat us just as much as anyone else and we'd never know it. I don't particularly care if he goes or stays . . . but I'm convinced that it won't be very comfortable having him in the same house! He doesn't like any of us . . . that's very obvious. And I can't say that I care much for him!'

'You must admit that he's a bit grim,' Rowena interjected.

Vanessa turned swiftly. 'Wouldn't you feel grim if someone was walking off with everything you held dear?'

'You certainly have taken up the cudgels for him,' Fiona remarked cuttingly. 'You seem more concerned for his feelings than ours, anyway.'

'We stand to gain a great deal . . . he loses everything,' Vanessa retorted.

'That isn't our fault!'

'No . . . but we don't have to treat him like a leper!'

'Well, I agree with Vanessa,' Belinda said stoutly. 'I don't know what all the fuss is about. I took it for granted he would go on living here and looking after the estate—and I think it's an excellent arrangement.' She dimpled mischievously. 'After all, he's rather attractive.'

'Don't be stupid!' Fiona said irritably. 'He must be twice your age and any fool can see that you bore him to tears with your play-acting!'

'Thanks very much! I haven't noticed that he's very smitten with you, either—that must be a blow to your ego! That probably explains why you're so offhand with him!'

'For heaven's sake!' Vanessa could not believe that these quarrelsome, petty-minded, infantile girls were the same girls who had lived together so amicably and happily in the past. She just didn't understand that they could change so much in such a short time—and she could not help wishing Fairlands, the money and Justin Fairgarth at the bottom of the ocean! 'Must you bicker like six year olds?'

'Isn't it rather silly to argue over such things just yet?' Melissa asked, almost shyly, having listened to the exchange with distress in her eyes. 'It may be ages yet before the legal business is settled—and really we need Mr. Fairgarth's help and advice. I agree he's a bit stand-offish but perhaps we're a bit too much for anyone—five of us, all strangers and all girls at that! I don't mean to dislike him without reason, anyway . . . he's been courteous and kind to me and I can't help feeling a bit sorry for him, too.'

Belinda laughed. 'Three to two, Fiona! You lose! Just because you're the eldest, it doesn't mean that you can make decisions by yourself. Fairlands belongs to all of us equally . . . and I suggest that we all agree now to discuss any matter that comes up and vote on it fairly.'

'Yes, that's true,' Rowena said quickly. 'You were a bit hasty, Fiona . . . after all, you didn't talk it over with us and we have the right to decide whether we want Mr. Fairgarth to manage the estate or not.'

'You've been sweeping about, giving yourself airs, ever since Thursday,' Belinda jeered. 'You didn't come into Fairlands on your own, you know.'

Fiona, flushed, her eyes stormy, walked into the room she had appropriated for herself and slammed the door.

'That was unnecessary, Belinda!' Vanessa

snapped.

Belinda shrugged. 'It was the truth.'

'Maybe . . . but it's applicable to all of you. I feel as if I've been living with four strangers since Thursday . . . and the sooner you revert to normal the better I shall like it! I wish Sir Wilfrid Fairgarth and Fairlands had never existed!'

'Phooey! You'll like having money and queening it as much as any of us!' Belinda retorted.

'Which just proves how little you really know about me—and how uninterested you are in my feelings in the matter!' she said tartly and walked along the hall to take her case from Justin as he reached the head of the stairs.

Alone in the room to which he had escorted her, with the air of ignoring her sisters' views on the matter, she sank down on the bed. Thoughts of the future had no pleasure for her as she reviewed that senseless squabbling between her sisters. She did not understand the potent powers of money and land . . . why their unexpected fortune should have turned their heads so easily and so swiftly.

They were full of plans for the future and they could talk of nothing but the money and what it would mean to them, the way of life they meant to follow, the clothes, the jewels, the furs, the fast cars, the parties and the nightclubs, the new friends, the luxuries and extravagances. They could not understand that it all left Vanessa completely unmoved. They could not understand that she longed to turn back the clock, that she would rather know the old ways for the rest of her life than face the changes that the new ways must inevitably bring. Within a few days she was out of touch with her sisters—and it was the knowledge that they would no longer need her which filled her with so much resentment and bitterness.

She had 'mothered' them gladly in a thousand ways, content in their affection and their dependence on her. Soon they would be no longer dependent . . . they would have maids to look after their clothes, to tidy their rooms, to help them to dress for an evening out . . . they would discard anything that needed a stitch rather than run to Vanessa with it . . . they would eat delicious food cooked and served by reliable, well-trained staff and Vanessa's culinary efforts would never be needed again.

She was shocked to realise how much importance each of them placed on money and what it could buy. She was disappointed that their dreams had apparently flown out of the window now that they could so easily be realised.

Fiona scorned the idea that she should open her own dress salon now that she could spend her life in a continual round of enjoyment. She would design her own clothes, she said airily—and after eight years of drudgery in a shop that was as much as she wanted to do!

Rowena impatiently dismissed the suggestion of the Slade . . . she would continue to paint, of course, there would be plenty of inspiration in new surroundings but it was no longer necessary for her to earn a living as an artist and she saw no reason to devote the best years of her life to art when she could be having a good time.

Melissa had her music at her finger-tips, she claimed . . . she would have the best piano that money could buy, but as she doubted her ability to attain the concert platform there was no point in studying with the famous teachers. She meant to enjoy herself now that she no longer had to play nursemaid to those wretched children.

Belinda would go on with her acting, of course . . . but *not* with the Benjamin Players. With her looks and acting ability and the influential people she was certain to meet once she was moving in the best circles she was bound to have many offers to appear in the West End.

Vanessa had listened to them with a sinking heart and swiftly realised the futility of offering any advice or suggestions. They would go their own way regardless of anything she might say . . . and they would not thank her for the 'interference'.

Perhaps she was making too much of the whole thing. Perhaps they would settle down once this first excitement died and it was likely that they would become so bored with the social round and lazy self-indulgence that they would gladly renew their former ambitions.

But, in any case, her own future seemed to stretch emptily before her. Since their mother's death her life had been full and busy and worthwhile and she had done her utmost to ensure that none of them suffered because of their loss. Now she felt lost and purposeless. Now she could not imagine how she would spend the days. Fairlands had a very competent housekeeper and a handful of servants to ensure its smooth running. She had no plans for wild orgies of shopping, for filling her days with social engagements or enjoying the enforced idleness. She did not ride: her tennis was very poor; she had never cared for cards. Nightclubs and theatres and restaurants held little appeal. Naturally shy and reserved, she did not look forwad to parties as her sisters did: the thought of moving in a new and unfamiliar society filled her with dread. It seemed to Vanessa that much of her time would be spent in her own company . . . and she feared boredom rather than solitude.

It was not surprising that she could not

think very kindly of Justin Fairgarth, quick though she had been to defend him, angry though she had been with Fiona for her callous attitude to his position. She could not forget that his advent into her life had brought nothing but problems and despondency to date . . . and she could not bring herself to be at ease with him, to offer the hand of friendship. It was not his fault—and she sensed that their existence did not please him any more than the unexpected fortune had pleased her. He had lost far more because Sir Wilfrid had failed to leave a will and she could feel a certain compassion for the man . . . until something reminded her forcibly of the change in her sisters and then she was utterly devoid of all feeling but that of bitter resentment.

CHAPTER EIGHT

Justin had invited Morny and Raif Fitzgerald to dinner and as the time approached for their arrival he found himself watching the clock anxiously.

He had spent the afternoon driving the Clements about the estate in his car and felt that he had already had more than his fill of them. It would be a relief when the Fitzgeralds were present to share the burden of conversation.

He greeted Morny with far more warmth than he would normally express and introduced Raif to the Clements with the air of one who gladly handed over the responsibility for entertaining them. Raif was a tall, handsome young man, something of a playboy and a very accomplished flirt. He very soon drifted to Fiona's side and monopolised her attention and she was not averse to a mild flirtation with the attractive man who contrasted so forcibly with the quiet, somewhat dour Justin Fairgarth.

Melissa was at the piano, idly strumming the notes of a medley of popular songs. Rowena and Belinda were talking, their conversation interspersed by gales of laughter, their curious glances frequently turning to the Fitzgeralds. Vanessa was standing by the window, her drink in her hand, surveying the room and its occupants with thoughtful eyes. Justin glanced at her and his eyes narrowed with impatience at that air of withdrawal and, he thought irritably, obvious boredom.

'What's wrong, darling?' Morny handed him her glass for a second cocktail. 'Have they been giving you a bad time?'

'I am a bit frayed at the edges,' he admitted.

'That isn't surprising. You've never cared much for the undiluted company of women.'

He smiled down at her. 'Not en masse, I agree. But there's a lot to be said for the company of one woman—particularly when she's very lovely.'

Morny glanced around the room. 'Which one in particular?'

'Don't be obtuse, my sweet,' he said lightly. He added: 'Nice of you to come at such short notice, Morny.'

'Wild horses couldn't have kept me away. I've been most curious about your unsuspected cousins, darling.'

'And what do you think of them at first glance?'

'A very attractive collection. Raif, you will have noticed, with his unerring eye has made a beeline for the most attractive. She's really a very striking woman, darling.'

'I admire his courage. She's been freezing me all day.'

She glanced at him obliquely through her lashes. 'And that annoys you?'

Justin smiled. 'Not exactly . . . but her manner is rather coldly offensive at times. Not only has she kindly offered me a job as estate manager at a salary that will be "worth my while" but she has also contrived to remind me quite pointedly, without actual words, that I am not lucky enough to have the rich royal blood of the Fairgarths in my veins.'

'Damnably offensive, I would say,' she said

with some heat. 'I hope you didn't accept her generous offer.'

He met her eyes steadily. 'You know my views, Morny.'

'Yes . . . that means that they won't be selling Fairlands, I gather.'

'It doesn't seem likely. Vanessa seems to be the only one in favour of selling. The others seem determined to move in at the earliest moment . . . they are already treating the place as though they've lived all their lives here.'

The bitterness in his tone caused her to look at him with warm compassion. 'No wonder you're feeling frayed at the edges. Which one is Vanessa?'

'In the green dress . . . standing by the window.'

Morny studied her for a long moment. 'She looks very aloof. No, darling, I can't say that I've taken to any of them so far . . .'

Belinda came to join them at that moment, making no secret of her wish to break up a tête-à-tête that she found unpalatable. 'Is this a private conversation or can anyone join in?' she asked lightly.

Her smile held a faint challenge as she met Morny's eyes and the older woman was conscious of a flicker of amusement. Did this pretty chit really hope to interest Justin? She would do well to learn less obvious tactics.

'You're Belinda . . . is that right?'

'The actress in the family,' Justin said smoothly.

Belinda threw him a swift, suspicious glance but found nothing in his expression to confirm the faint mockery of his tone.

'How interesting! Are you appearing in a production at the moment?'

'I'm resting just now . . . by my own choice, of course,' she hastened to add.

'Justin was just saying that you've decided not to sell Fairlands,' Morny volunteered pleasantly.

Belinda widened her eyes. 'Was there any doubt about it? It's our family home . . . of course we won't sell. I'm looking forward to living in this lovely house with its echo of family ghosts.'

Morny bravely suppressed a smile. 'We shall be neighbours . . . Raif and I live at Tay Court on the other side of the village.'

With a murmured excuse, Justin left them and crossed the room to speak to Vanessa. She glanced up at his approach, having sat down on the padded window seat.

'May I get you a drink?' he asked courteously.

'No, thank you.' She raised her glass to show him its contents. 'I haven't finished this yet.'

'Don't you care for cocktails? Would you prefer sherry?'

She shook her head. 'I'm quite all right.'

He sat down by her side. 'Fiona seems to have made a conquest,' he said lightly.

'Yes, so it seems,' she returned, a little doubtfully, glancing at Raif's tall figure.

'He's extremely impressionable and a shocking flirt but harmless enough,' he said reassuringly.

'Fiona can take care of herself,' she replied coolly.

'I'm sure she can . . . but you looked a little anxious,' he told her lightly.

Vanessa was disconcerted. 'Did I? I don't think Fiona was on my mind.'

'I wonder what you were thinking?' He smiled easily, guided by the wish to put her at her ease rather than curiosity.

She turned to him and her eyes met his frankly. 'I was wondering how to explain to you that Fiona doesn't mean to be quite so outspoken. I'm sure she offended you this morning—and I'm sorry that she was so tactless. I don't think she realised that there isn't any question of you having to leave Fairlands unless you wish . . . and really we should all be most grateful to you if you continued to manage the estate for us.' It was a long speech that left her rather breathless. It was also rather difficult to make with those cynical, mocking eyes holding her own.

'All of you?' he asked quietly. 'I wonder . . .'

'You will stay, won't you?' The colour was

rapidly staining her cheeks.

'Oh, I don't think so,' he said carelessly. 'This is my opportunity to try fresh fields—and I've been at Fairlands too long, anyway.'

'You *are* offended,' she said bluntly.

He shrugged. 'Perhaps.'

'I'm sorry . . .' she began but he cut her short.

'I don't expect you to apologise for your sister,' he said curtly.

Unexpectedly she laughed. 'Well, don't expect an apology from Fiona . . . it wouldn't be in character. She always sails on as though nothing has happened and is most surprised to find that the other person is remembering an incident she has completely forgotten.'

'Thank you for that brief insight into Fiona's character—but I doubt that it will be necessary. We won't be seeing very much of each other in the future.'

Dismay touched her eyes. 'But you must always think of Fairlands as your home!'

His expression softened a little. 'That's very good of you, Vanessa.'

'Please don't be sarcastic . . . I mean it,' she said swiftly. 'Perhaps I phrased it rather badly . . . obviously this will always be your home . . . I only meant that I'd hate to think that we'd driven you away. I know we must be rather overwhelming and . . .' she looked down at her glass in embarrassment, 'I suppose you think that we are all very lacking in manners. But this is very exciting to us, you know—and it's knocked us a little off balance.'

'Yes, I know that feeling,' he said grimly.

There was something in his tone that brought back in a sudden surge all the antagonism he so easily provoked. 'Well, it isn't our fault!' she flared. 'I do think you might try to be a little more gracious . . . heaven knows we didn't want Fairlands or the wretched money! We were quite content as we were!'

'You're speaking for the Clements as a whole, of course,' he said mockingly and in obvious disbelief.

'At least I'm speaking for myself . . . and I'm sure my sisters will feel the same when they get over the first shock and excitement!' she retorted indignantly.

He nodded. 'I'm convinced that you would prefer to spend your days pounding a typewriter in a dingy city office . . . it's so obviously your natural surroundings. You are like a fish out of water here . . . even if your sisters display all the ennui and easy acceptance of those who've lived in luxury since they were born.'

Her eyes were cold. 'Miss Fitzgerald is trying to attract your attention . . . please don't neglect your friends. You will have plenty of opportunities to be as unpleasant as you wish to me and my sisters.'

He rose abruptly to his feet. 'You make it easy for me to retaliate in kind,' he snapped. 'Your attitude to the whole business is not only offensive . . . but extremely incredible! Please don't feel that you must pretend to be sorry about this affair for my sake—you're welcome to Fairlands with my best wishes. By the time you and your sisters have "improved" it here and there, it won't be worth the having!' He turned on his heel and strode back to the bar, pale, tense and extremely angry.

Vanessa's knuckles were white with strain as she gripped her hands in an effort at self-control. She had provoked his anger, it was true . . . but she was growing a little weary at his failure to hide his chagrin and resentment and she told herself that he was man enough to accept the circumstances and cut out the self-pity. Did he think it was going to be a bed of roses for her in the future?

She abruptly realised, with a tiny shock, that she was refusing to accept the circumstances and that she had done little but feel sorry for herself since the news had broken. So her sisters would no longer need her—but there were other compensations. Her future life would only be as empty as she allowed it to be. There were many things she could take an interest in . . . she might even

111

study estate management so that eventually she could take over the reins herself!

She had been blaming Justin Fairgarth unfairly: it was not his fault that he was merely an adopted son and therefore ineligible to inherit the estate; it was not his fault that she and her sisters had been thrust into this new way of life. He could not be blamed for the ways her sisters were behaving . . . and it was not surprising that he thought her as eager and excited as they were and despised her 'pretence'. He did not know her: how could he tell whether or not she was sincere; why should she expect him to know how she was really feeling?

She glanced across the room. He had rapidly recovered himself and was smiling down at Morny Fitzgerald while she talked to him. They seemed to be on excellent terms, she thought with a strange flicker of resentment—and then reminded herself that they had been friends and neighbours for years. Naturally they were on easy terms: naturally he would prefer her company to that of the strangers who had given him such a difficult day. She was not making it easier for him by giving back hostility for hostility, unpleasantness for unpleasantness, resentment for resentment.

She was usually such a placid person that the swift, fierce anger he evoked so easily left her feeling shaken and a little sick. She had always believed that a gentle answer turned away wrath and the family had always called her the 'little peacemaker'. Instead of adding fuel to the odd, unreasonable feud between him and her sisters, it would be much better if she concentrated her energies on trying to make a peace between them. He was possibly a very likeable person if one could only break through the barrier of antagonism he had erected. In any case, stranger though he might be, he was a member of their family, no matter what Fiona might think. It said little for their tolerance and generosity if they could not accept him as such and show him friendliness and warmth . . .

'You were getting very heated,' Belinda said lightly. 'What on earth was all that about?'

She started, so deep in thought that she had not noticed her sister's approach. 'Oh . . . nothing much! I was merely trying to explain that we hoped he would stay and look after things for us.'

Belinda raised an incredulous eyebrow. 'Excusing Fiona, you mean,' she said shrewdly. 'He turned you down, of course.'

'I'm not sure . . . he said something about fresh fields.'

Belinda laughed. 'Probably he plans to buy a few more acres and make a nice little profit on the side.'

'Don't talk like that about him!' Vanessa

snapped. 'You'll have to learn to live with him if he stays—and it won't help if you allow Fiona to poison your mind against him!'

'Yes . . . what does she have against him, anyway?' Belinda asked, puzzled. 'Apart from his obvious lack of interest in her charms, I mean.'

Vanessa shrugged. 'One of her unreasonable dislikes, I suppose.'

'I didn't think you liked him much yourself.'

'I scarcely know him,' Vanessa retorted pointedly.

'Perhaps he improves with knowing . . . he really is awfully attractive, Van,' she added in a lower tone. 'It seems a pity that he doesn't smile more often—as he's smiling now.'

Vanessa reluctantly followed her gaze—and met Justin's eyes across the room. His smile was for something that Morny had said and he had glanced unconsciously in Vanessa's direction. It was a warm, kindly smile and genuine laughter touched his eyes . . . and something strange, unknown, almost unwelcome yet oddly thrilling twisted in her heart. She looked away hastily, her heart pounding in her throat.

'I expect Miss Fitzgerald thinks he's very attractive, too,' she said tartly . . . and was relieved that dinner was announced at that moment. The startled hint of perception in Belinda's eyes was more than

114

disconcerting . . .

Raif devoted himself almost exclusively to Fiona and she was very animated and very lovely . . . and very offhand with Justin. It was hard work for him, left to entertain five women on his own, and he wished he had invited a few more men although it would have entailed a bigger dinner-party than he had wished.

It was easier when the meal was finished and they returned to the drawing-room. Melissa needed little persuasion to play for them and they settled themselves comfortably with only the soft lighting of the wall lamps, the steady flames of the log fire and the standard lamp by the piano to bring an atmosphere of intimacy into the room. Raif reluctantly detached himself from Fiona, having been told in no uncertain terms by his host and good friend that he was of damned little use in easing the awkwardness of the evening. He sat between Rowena and Belinda and set himself out to be attentive while Morny drew Fiona into low-toned conversation. Justin provided drinks and cigarettes and then, confident that his guests were all settled, went to stand by the piano.

Melissa smiled at him shyly but she was so absorbed in her music that she scarcely knew at whom she smiled. She had a wonderful gift and a perfect touch and Justin was speedily lost to everything but the music.

Vanessa rose quietly from her seat, a little apart from the others, and went as silently from the room. In her bedroom, she took a cigarette from her case and held a match to it with hands that trembled slightly. She had still not recovered from the shock of meeting Justin's laughing eyes across the room . . . and she sat down abruptly and covered her own eyes with her hands as though to erase the image so clearly etched there. It was ridiculous, incredible, utterly foolish. Did she really imagine that love could come in a flash like that . . . completely out of the blue, totally unexpected, utterly unwelcome? Sheer fantasy! Love was born of long friendship, of gradually deepening affection, of quiet, easy knowledge and acceptance of each other's ways and feelings and thoughts. Never like this! She would not admit the fierce tumult of heart and mind to be proof of a love that shattered her quiet, placid existence.

Bad enough to be tumbled out of her accepted, contented way of life without warning . . . but to fall in love like a silly schoolgirl with a man so supremely indifferent, so harshly antagonistic was the worst thing that could have happened to her!

She did not dare to indulge the odd fancy but had to make up her mind to fight it, no matter what it cost. As if Justin Fairgarth would ever look twice in her direction! Any fool could see that he was in love with Morny

116

Fitzgerald—and any woman would be a fool if she thought she could compete with Morny's attractions and lively high spirits. The woman had a flying head start over her and any other girl who fancied herself in love with the man she obviously meant to have for her own eventually . . .

Vanessa sat on the edge of her bed, troubled by turbulent thoughts and emotions she could scarcely control, until she was chilled and weary . . . until Melissa burst into the room, exclaiming her relief at having found her missing sister.

'What are you doing up here, anyway? We've all been quite anxious about you! Heaven knows what the Fitzgeralds will think of you—sneaking out like that! And they're so nice, too. Are you all right?' she added on a suddenly urgent note, realising Vanessa's pallor and the strange darkness of her eyes.

'Yes . . . perfectly,' she said with an effort and rose, aware of stiffness and coldness in her bones.

'Justin sent me to find you . . . he seemed quite worried about you,' Melissa volunteered.

So they were on first name terms now, Vanessa thought bitterly . . . was that for the Fitzgeralds' benefit or had he thawed a little once she was out of the way?

'I don't give a damn whether he was worried or not!' she said vehemently and with complete disregard for the truth . . . and followed her sister reluctantly from the room.

CHAPTER NINE

Justin could scarcely settle to anything during those difficult weeks of waiting. He seemed to have lost all his interest in the estate now that he no longer felt he was working for his own benefit in the long run. Why should he care if the estate was run at a loss or if it showed a satisfactory profit? He would get no thanks from the Clements in either case.

They were only interested in the money which would enable them to live in luxury for the rest of their lives. City girls: how could he expect them to be interested in the home farm, the herd of pedigree cattle, the flock of new lambs, the necessity to buy a new bull, the state of the fences, the new farm machinery that he had ordered? Their empty heads turned only to thoughts of clothes and jewels and fast cars.

He failed to understand why they wanted to keep Fairlands. The house . . . he could appreciate that they thought of it as the perfect setting for them and an excellent address to boost their entry into society. And it spared them the problem of finding a suitable house to throw open to their friends.

He had suggested that they should sell at least some of the land but he had met with unexpected opposition from Vanessa, of all people. The others had not seemed to care much one way or the other, Fiona's only interest displayed by a pertinent query as to the amount of money the land would fetch.

He had never seen Vanessa quite so determined. She had flayed her sisters' apathy with scorn in eyes and voice—and then turned the tide of her anger on him, making it very clear that she would not sanction the sale of one acre of the estate. Fiona had shrugged her indifference to the matter: Belinda had sided with Vanessa—as, he had noticed, she usually did when issues were raised; Melissa and Rowena had scarcely contributed to the discussion and it was obvious that they were ignorant of any importance attaching to the land.

He did not know that Vanessa's refusal stemmed from her knowledge of his love for every acre of the land that had been his primary interest for so long. While she had breath in her body, she would not allow anyone to despoil one part of the estate which she always thought of as Justin's rightful heritage. Nor did he know that she meant to devote her time and energies to learning as much as she could about the management of the estate in order to share his interest.

He was merely astonished by her

vehemence and completely at a loss to understand it. He doubted very much that the blood of the Fairgarths, landowners and lovers of the land for generations, stirred so strongly in her veins that it was an instinctive protest against his suggestion.

Justin had not changed his mind about leaving Fairlands—and his strange lack of interest of late merely served to confirm the belief that he could never be happy working for the Clements. As soon as it could be arranged, he meant to shake the earth of Fairlands from his feet and set out on a new and different path. He had a man in mind to take his place and young John Byfield did not need any persuasion. In fact, he could scarcely believe his good luck or that the offer was genuine. To be estate manager of Fairlands was far more than he had ever dared to hope . . . but Justin, knowing his background and character and having followed with interest his management of Sir William Worth's land, bordering on Fairlands but a much smaller estate, was confident that Byfield could step into his shoes and do the job admirably.

From time to time, during the past weeks, huge boxes had arrived at the house from famous couturiers and equally famous London stores. A trunk full of books and paintings had also arrived. At every visit the Clements brought a few of their personal possessions and installed them in the rooms they had commandeered—constant reminders that they would soon be taking over the house and that he would be looking for a job and finding his feet in new surroundings.

Fiona had brought two precious young men to the house—men whose clothes and voices grated unbearably on Justin. It transpired that they were experts in the field of interior décor and that Fiona wanted them to do what they could to make Fairlands 'habitable'. Justin gritted his teeth and suppressed an instinctive protest. To him, the house had always been perfect . . . a little shabby, perhaps, but homely and comfortable and welcoming. Fiona's open contempt for the furniture and furnishings was hurtful and, he thought, unnecessarily premature. When they had taken possession and he was well out of the way, they could do as they liked: until the legalities were settled, he would have thought more kindly of her if she had bided her time. He was even more convinced that it would be intolerable for him to remain at Fairlands. He could imagine what the house would look like by the time Fiona and her odd friends had finished with it!

Belinda arrived unexpectedly with a carload of her friends one afternoon. They were a very theatrical crowd, over-dressed and excitable, too ready to gush and exclaim over everything. This he could have borne

. . . but it was too much to realise that Belinda was claiming him as her personal property and had even hinted to her friends that she was virtually engaged to him. He snubbed her mercilessly, left her friends in no doubt that their heavy congratulations and coy comments were not only premature but exceedingly misplaced and walked out of the house in a grim fury. It was unlikely that Belinda would ever forgive him—but her dislike and annoyance were infinitely preferable to her clinging and possessive airs.

Melissa and Rowena made several visits—and Justin wondered with wry amusement if one ever did anything without the other. They seemed inseparable, might as well have been the twins that many people believed them to be, and seemed to need each other as much for moral support as anything else. Melissa came to spend hours at the piano: Rowena could be found in odd corners of the grounds with her easel and palette. Justin became quite used to seeing them about the place and soon accepted their quiet, shy presence. They were certainly no trouble to him or anyone else: indeed, they seemed awed and afraid of him and scarcely spoke except to hope that they weren't being a nuisance. It was almost as though they expected him to grow a pair of horns at any moment and batter them with demoniac fury, he sometimes thought impatiently.

Vanessa did not visit Fairlands. It was almost as though she refused to admit that the place had anything to do with her or that she had any interest in it at all. He had only seen her once since that disastrous weekend when antagonism and arguments had been rife—and that was the day he travelled to London to learn their views on selling some of the land.

He had been vaguely surprised to discover that she was working out a month's notice with Hardy and Bamber for her sisters had left their jobs as soon as they learned of their good fortune. Although Vanessa seemed to have dropped her hostile attitude to him, he could not help feeling that she disliked him. She was so stiff and formal, so withdrawn, so silent except when it was necessary to speak and then she made her remarks as brief as courtesy allowed. He thought her very ill at ease—and it was even more marked when they were alone for a few moments. She had risen from her chair and walked aimlessly about the room, returning a book to the shelf, straightening a picture on the wall, plumping a cushion, picking up a magazine and leafing through it absently. He had tried to talk to her but she had made conversation impossible with her taciturn replies and frequent distractions. He had lapsed into silence, feeling irritated by her gaucherie. It had been a relief when Fiona returned with cigarettes and the offer of a drink . . .

The Clements were spending money like water—and Justin scanned the rapidly-incoming bills with a grim expression before setting them aside to be paid when he did the monthly accounts.

Fiona had bought a shocking pink and white sports car and a complete outfit to match it. Furs and expensive hats and shoes, a diamond bracelet, a diamond dress ring with its vulgarly large stone, masses of flimsy lingerie, evening gowns and tailored suits, a complete set of travelling cases and a beautifully-fitted dressing case were just a few of the items on the bills which she had signed so casually—and which had been sent to him as they had agreed.

Belinda had also bought a car—a small pale blue coupé—and was having a course of driving lessons. She had not been quite so extravagant as Fiona but nevertheless Justin wondered when she would wear all the suits and dresses that she had ordered. Most of the money she spent seemed to be on parties for her friends at famous hotels and nightclubs—and Justin wondered wryly if she had realised the extent of her popularity before she became so wealthy.

Melissa had ordered a grand piano from the most famous instrument makers in the world and it was due to arrive any day. She and Rowena had also indulged in a vast shopping spree . . . and Rowena seemed to be spending time and money in encouraging unknown artists at exorbitant prices, judging by the quality of the paintings which had arrived in a batch.

It struck him for the first time that there had not been one bill signed by Vanessa. Did she prefer to wait until the money was actually theirs rather than draw on the estate in the meantime? Or was it merely a rather foolish gesture of independence? He could not believe that she was so indifferent to all that money could buy!

They were wealthy young women, it was true, but the estate could not stand a continual drain on its resources to such an extent. He realised that he would have to explain to them that forty thousand pounds was soon spent at the rate they were spending—and that Fairlands had to be maintained at the same time. One could not keep taking money away from the land, it was a continual business of putting money into it if they wished to maintain their income. He appreciated that this initial splurge was perfectly natural and would not last but it would be as well to warn them to moderate their spending in the future.

Fiona had very nearly exhausted her share of the income for the year and he doubted that she would take kindly to the news that she had little over a thousand pounds left to her account. He was determined not to pay for their extravagances out of the estate fund—he only hoped they would be sensible enough to continue his arrangement of setting aside a fairly large portion of the annual income towards the running of Fairlands. The income from farm produce, the sale of beef and lamb, the leasing of grazing land and fishing rights were not sufficient to run a large estate like Fairlands without assistance in these days of heavy taxation and high prices. Fortunately the capital was wisely invested and there was a great deal of property which made a high percentage of the Fairgarth fortune.

Whether or not the Clements would advise Clifford Gantry, the estate broker, sensibly and practically as one must hope, remained to be seen. Cliff had a wise head on his shoulders: he was a very firm man, astute and reliable; Justin did not think he would be easily swayed by the Clements no matter how great their powers of persuasion.

He was very busy, despite the heaviness of his heart. For he was quite determined that the Clements should have no reason to accuse him of neglecting estate affairs since their arrival on the scene. There was always plenty to keep him occupied, manually and mentally, and all unconsciously he was setting the estate in perfect order in readiness of his successor. John Byfield would need time to adjust himself to the demands made on him by Fairlands: it would not help if he had to deal with overdue accounts and overlooked matters.

The next time Fiona made one of her flying visits to Fairlands, he broached the subject of John Byfield.

'He's very keen, a capable and competent man. He's had two years estate management at an agricultural college so he probably knows more than I do about the business. For the past year he's been with Sir William and I gather that the place is paying its way for the first time in years. You won't do badly to have Byfield in my place—and I'm prepared to work with him for a month or so to help him over the first hurdles.'

He had asked Fiona to come into the study, the room which was more his own than any other room in the house. It was very masculine without being austere: bookcases lined one wall; the windows overlooked the well-kept gardens. The rich red of carpet and heavy drapes gave the room warmth and vitality and the big desk with its piles of folders and papers, its two telephones and its neat stack of reference books indicated that it was a room for work rather than relaxation.

Fiona leaned forward to accept the cigarette he offered, her expression faintly amused. 'You've never forgiven me, have you?' she asked lightly.

He flicked a lighter to life and she bowed her head over the flame, steadying his hand with the gentle yet meaningless pressure of her slender fingers.

He was deliberately obtuse. 'Forgiven you? I'm afraid I'm not with you . . .'

Her smile widened. 'Exactly—you're deserting us, Justin. Rather unkind and unnecessary, don't you think? Is it fair to leave us to the mercies of a stranger who probably knows as little as we do about running a big estate like Fairlands?'

He shrugged, struggling with annoyance. 'Kindness and fairness don't come into it. Byfield is very capable,' he repeated. 'And he has had training in estate management.'

'And you can't wait to escape from the den of iniquity that Fairlands will surely become in our hands?' Her eyes mocked him.

He rose impatiently. 'What you do with Fairlands is not my concern! If you are not in the mood to discuss this sensibly, we'd better leave it until another day.'

'But there isn't much time left, is there? I'm informed that the business should be finalised next week—and I'm sure you want to get this settled and make your own plans for the future,' she said sweetly.

'Well, I recommend Byfield . . . you must decide if you want to give him a trial,' he said curtly.

'I don't care what you do—as long as you

can assure me that this man won't play ducks and drakes with our money,' she retorted. 'You say he's reliable and trustworthy and knows his job . . . very well. Engage him.' She moved her slim shoulders in a faint shrug. 'I'm sure we don't want to interfere with your plans in any way. You're perfectly welcome to stay on as estate manager—or go your own way, as you please. Just remember that it's your own choice—and we have no intention of feeling guilty because you've no longer any say in how Fairlands is run. Is that clear?' Her tone was peremptory now and a little hard.

Justin looked at her steadily and with dislike. In her eyes, he was a nobody. It meant nothing to her that he had been virtually the son of the house for many years, that everyone, including himself, had expected him to be Sir Wilfrid's heir, that he had a certain right to consider Fairlands as his own. She merely thought of him as an employee of the estate, a difficult and hostile employee, and it mattered nothing whether he went or stayed. Damn the entire pack of Clements! Heaven knew he had no reason to like any one of them.

He did not want sympathy or concern for his position—but if he had been desperate for them, he would still have been denied them! Was it too much to expect a little friendliness, a little warmth, a little of the milk of human kindness in their dealings with him?

Belinda had been friendly, it was true—but only to her own mysterious ends and now he had offended her irrevocably. Melissa and Rowena were as wary of him as though he were a raging fiend. Vanessa could not be bothered with him at all . . . and Fiona had trampled on his feelings from the very beginning.

Well, they could have Fairlands and the money and be damned to them all! Much happiness they would find beneath the roof which was used to shelter warm and kindly people with generous hearts and purses! The house knew how to offer a welcome—and how to discourage those with selfish, cold hearts and minds.

Fanciful thoughts, perhaps—but the self mockery did not rid him of the conviction that Fairlands would bring heartache and humiliation to the strangers within its gates.

'You always make your meaning very clear,' he said harshly. 'Thank you for giving me your time.' He turned back to his desk where he had spent so many gladly-given hours on the estate affairs.

Fiona sat still for a moment, looking at his uncompromising back as he turned over a sheaf of papers. She sensed his anger but did not accept that she had said anything to incur it. She had always been blunt and outspoken, even tactless—but always she had been forgiven because of her vital personality. It was something new to be disliked as violently as Justin Fairgarth disliked her—a little disconcerting to be addressed so harshly and dismissed so abruptly.

He was a remarkably handsome man . . . it was a pity his manners left so much to be desired . . . a pity he had set out to be unpleasant from the beginning. It was as well that he had made up his mind to go for she could imagine the arguments that would arise if he continued to manage the estate and was perhaps allowed to fancy that he was the sole authority on its affairs.

She rose and smoothed her skirt. 'We're giving a cocktail party at the flat next week to celebrate—Thursday at six-thirty. You'll come, of course.'

'No, thank you. I have too much to do at the moment and cocktail parties were never much in my line,' he replied coldly.

'I thought you'd be escorting Morny Fitzgerald. She and her brother are coming. I thought it good policy to get to know our neighbours well in advance.' There was subtle mockery in her tone.

'If Raif is going then his sister will scarcely need me to escort her,' he said curtly.

'Oh well . . . please yourself. I told Vanessa you wouldn't come but she insisted that you were to be asked,' she said carelessly, moving towards the door. She had no idea that if Vanessa had been present her remark would have given her sister every provocation for committing murder.

'Very nice of her,' he said shortly. 'Please convey my regrets.'

'Oh, I'll explain that the thought of the Clements en masse once more was just too much for you,' she retorted sweetly and strolled from the room in her elegant high heels.

Justin, understandably infuriated, seized a heavy paperweight and threw it across the room with forceful intent. It missed everything but a small table lamp that he had always detested—a long-ago present from Morny before her present good taste had been acquired.

The door opened. 'What on earth was that?' Fiona demanded. Then she saw the shattered pieces of the lamp and the paperweight a little beyond it. She laughed—a silvery, mocking laugh that made Justin long to lay hands on her. 'Temper, temper!' she gibed and closed the door on another provocative laugh . . .

CHAPTER TEN

The cocktail party was in full swing and Fiona, in a black velvet dress that came demurely to her throat while leaving her shoulders and slender back completely bare, was well pleased with its success, particularly as it had been her inspiration.

She was surrounded by a bevy of admirers and thoroughly enjoying herself, a drink in one hand, a cigarette in its long jet holder in the other, her eyes bright with vivacity and her mood completely attuned to the occasion.

The large room was crowded, each of them having invited several friends except for Vanessa who would have asked Maureen and her Stan if she had thought they would be at ease in this sophisticated company. Her only guest was Mr. Hardy who had accepted the invitation with alacrity and was at that very moment giving her fatherly advice as to the wisdom of investing her money in a company he could recommend without any qualms.

Vanessa listened politely but her attention was not really on his remarks. She glanced about the room with anxious eyes.

Belinda and her friends were scattered, very intent on recounting their experiences in the world of the theatre to anyone who would listen.

Melissa was talking earnestly to a pale, bespectacled young man who was talking with equal earnestness at the same time and conducting the tempo of their discussion with a cocktail stick, complete with its cherry, innocently unaware of the picture he made.

The rather arty young people, some in need of a haircut and a good wash, others obviously too poor to afford shirts and socks, were without a doubt the friends that Rowena had made during recent weeks—and their influence was beginning to affect her work which had suddenly developed a modernistic tendency.

Fiona's vivacious laugh cut across a small break in the babble of conversation and Vanessa turned to glance at her sister and the group of immaculately-dressed, admiring men.

Everyone was enjoying themselves—and Vanessa told herself brusquely that it was ridiculous for her to lack the party spirit merely because one man had not come to join the gaiety. He would not come now . . . it was past nine o'clock, beer and spirits had replaced the cocktails and it looked as though it would develop into the kind of party that went on all night and ended with a dozen or so unfamiliar faces appearing at the breakfast table.

Mr. Hardy was a crashing bore but there was no one else she wanted to be with and so she stood with him and murmured suitable monosyllables whenever he paused for breath. Vanessa saw Clifford Gantry standing alone and catching his eye, she beckoned him over to introduce him to Mr. Hardy. They might have something in common, if it was only stocks and shares, and she left them with a bright smile and a vague murmur.

She went out of the room, edged past an amorous couple on the stairs and made her way to her bedroom. She studied her reflection in the mirror, the shiny nose, the untidy hair, the smudged lipstick and the anxious eyes that looked back at her. She sat down and, with sudden determination, began to repair her make-up.

How stupid to consider her evening ruined because one man was not present! There were half a dozen men in the other room, all more attractive, more friendly, more likeable than Justin Fairgarth—and there was no point in snubbing advances for his sake!

Why had he turned down the invitation? He couldn't really be so busy. Did he want as little contact with them as possible? Did he resent them so much?

Soon they would leave this familiar, homely flat for Fairlands—and then it would only be a matter of weeks before Justin walked out of her life. Fiona had told them about John Byfield and Justin's eagerness to hand over the estate management. Vanessa did not blame him for wanting to get away—the future could only hold constant reminders of his loss and their gain. But why was he so averse to their friendship? And how could she find any measure of happiness, any peace of mind, knowing that she might never see him except by chance, knowing that only one man could ever mean anything to her—and that man the indifferent, hostile, difficult Justin Fairgarth who was determined to remain a stranger.

It was incredible that she should love him so much that every day was coloured by thoughts of him and every night disturbed by dreams of him. Why this man? What did she know of him? They had met only three or four times at the most. He had never given her cause to love him . . . why, that moment when their eyes met across the room and she knew that she had given her heart without encouragement, without invitation, without hope, he had been talking and laughing with another woman—and Vanessa knew, deep in her being, that he was in love with that woman. He would never have had a thought for her if circumstances had been different and they had met without the constant current of resentment and hostility. So her love for him was not only incredible—it was also the greatest folly she had ever committed and the sooner she dismissed him from her heart and mind the happier she would be!

He must dislike them all intensely if he had forgone an evening with Morny Fitzgerald rather than meet them on a social basis. Morny and Raif had been among the first arrivals and Vanessa had hurried to greet them, her heart hammering with hope. But her spirits had sunk beyond raising when she looked in vain for the tall figure of Justin in the background. She had swallowed her disappointment and welcomed the Fitzgeralds with pleasant warmth, taking pains to introduce them to those of the guests who would be most congenial to them . . .

Now, Raif was one of the group surrounding Fiona and the last she had seen of Morny was when she had been imprisoned in a corner by a determined young artist, apparently content and very much amused.

Vanessa liked the Fitzgeralds. They were an easy, amusing and friendly couple—and even her love for Justin could not persuade her into any feeling of jealousy or dislike towards Morny. It would not be surprising if Justin did care more for Morny than any other woman he knew—or if he had every intention of marrying her eventually. They were not engaged and Morny seemed to have a variety of men-friends . . . but one would need to be very lacking in perception not to sense the warm intimacy and affection that existed between Justin and the beautiful, sophisticated Morny Fitzgerald.

She would never be sophisticated, Vanessa thought, a little disconsolately. She was not the type. She was far happier planning and preparing a meal or turning out a room or stitching away happily at a piece of sewing than spending her days in an orgy of shopping or her nights in a round of social activity. The lazy indulgence and pampered extravagances of the wealthy did not appeal to her—and for one mad moment, she toyed with the idea of signing over her share of the income to her sisters, asking Mr. Hardy if she could have her job back, keeping on the flat and continuing in the way of life she knew and understood.

The impulse died very quickly. It was neither practical nor sincere. She could not afford this flat on her salary and it was much too big for one person: she could not face the prospect of a bed-sitting room or a small flatlet nor the thought of finding such a place; she had no real wish to resume the pounding of a typewriter, the poring over reams of legal documents, the hurrying with pad and pencil every time the buzzer summoned her to Mr. Hardy's office. It was true that she could keep her share of the money and keep the flat—and wave farewell to her sisters as they set off for Fairlands. But she continued to hope that one day they would recapture the old affinity and companionship, the need of each other, the warm sisterly intimacy . . . she had struggled to keep them together and it would be silly to allow them to drift now. For drift they would once the others were at Fairlands and living a life of luxury and being caught up in the whirl of new friendships and social engagements. They would soon forget to wonder how she

138

was faring—and how would she fare, on her own in London with only a few friends and without her sisters to share the problems and the pleasures, the family jokes, the elations and the desperations of everyday life.

She would go to Fairlands and make the best of the future. She did not have to spend her days in idleness: there must be a great many things she could do—and at least she could still be mother-confessor and general arbiter to her sisters as she had always been. They would still have their grumbles and their conquests—and there would always be arguments to settle . . .

She went back to the crowded living-room, returned a warm smile to the young man who caught her arm and gallantly handed her his glass, glanced over to see that Mr. Hardy and Clifford Gantry were deep in conversation and looked about her for a familiar face.

She caught her breath. That broad back, that crisp dark hair that clustered in small, curling tendrils at the nape of his neck, the familiar impatience of a sudden gesture—and, sufficiently convincing, the deep, pleasant voice that cut like a swathe through the babble of sound.

Vanessa realised that she was trembling. It was such a shock that he should have come when she had long given up hope! She looked at the glass in her hand and raised it to her lips, thinking the spirit might give back strength to her knees which seemed to have turned to jelly and warm the cold pit of sickness in her stomach. It was a very potent whisky and she tossed it off quickly before she realised what the glass contained. Then she choked, her throat on fire, the whisky searing its way through her slim body.

Justin turned. He gave her a cool little nod. 'Good evening . . . I'm afraid I'm rather late.'

'I thought you weren't coming,' she said rashly.

He raised a quizzical eyebrow. 'It's nice to be missed. As a matter of fact, I did turn down the invitation. But as I had to be in London today on business, I decided to stay overnight and it seemed rather ungracious not to join in your celebration.'

'You have nothing to celebrate.'

'Oh, I don't know . . . I think I've landed a very good job,' he said smoothly. 'My business was with Lord Stokes and I seem to have made quite a good impression—he has a big estate in Norfolk, you know, and I happened to hear that he needed a new manager.'

'Norfolk! But that's miles from Fairlands.'

'Yes . . . that must be quite a relief.' He took her glass. 'Let me get you a drink—and we can drink a toast to the future with a great many miles between us.' He turned away.

'Don't go, Justin,' she said recklessly.

He looked back. 'I'll be back in a minute

with your drink,' he said carelessly.

'I didn't mean that,' she blurted desperately.

He smiled down at her suddenly and unexpectedly. 'You've been mixing your drinks, my dear. What was this devil's brew, anyway?' He raised her glass to his nose and frowned. 'No wonder you choked . . . I don't rate you as a whisky-drinker.'

'No . . . I'm not. Someone gave it to me,' she stammered. 'I didn't mean to drink it.' She realised with horror that she was having difficulty in enunciating her words and that his face seemed to be looming towards her. But it was ridiculous . . . as if one whisky could have such an effect. And then she remembered the cocktails and the John Collins that she had been drinking during the evening.

Justin's hand was firm on her elbow, bringing a vivid memory of that first day of meeting when he had steered her along pavements with that merciless grip on her arm. 'Let's get out of this crush,' he said smoothly. 'It's absolutely stifling.'

She went with him weakly, vaguely noticed that more couples had commandeered the stairs but that they moved willingly for Justin's impressive build, stumbled at the head of the stairs and found herself clutching at him for support.

'Where are we going?' she pleaded,

wanting only to crawl with her humiliation into her room and bury her hot, shamed face in the pillows of her bed.

'To get you some fresh air,' he said firmly.

The door of the house was open to the night air for the convenience of their guests . . . and they had wisely invited the students from the flat below to the party so there could be no complaints in the morning.

Vanessa leaned against the railing and took deep breaths of the chill, reassuring air. Her head seemed to clear a little . . . and then she realised that Justin's arm was about her shoulders and that stupid trembling began again.

'I . . . feel such a fool,' she stammered.

'No need,' he returned crisply. 'It happens to everyone at sometime or the other—and it isn't so very terrible.'

'Oh, isn't it?' she retorted and he laughed.

'You'll be all right in a few minutes. Keep quiet and breathe deeply. Don't be silly about it . . . don't even think of giving in to the muzziness in your head.' His tone was firm and imperative and it was instinctive to do as she was told.

He was so close—she could feel his warm breath on her cheek and the reassuring strength of his arm. There was a faint, male scent of after-shave in her nostrils and the smooth material of his suit brushing her hair. She closed her eyes . . . a fatal move for her head swam and she leaned against him involuntarily. He steadied her with his other arm and now she could feel the steady rhythm of his heart against the softness of her body and a strange, sensuous excitement stirred in her veins. She raised her face and met his dark, smiling eyes . . . her heart was pounding so furiously in her throat that it must betray the turbulent emotion within her but she did not care in that moment. Neither of them made that first, instinctive movement—and yet somehow their lips met and clung for a long moment. Vanessa was only conscious of an involuntary wonder at the sweetness of his kiss as her lips parted beneath the pressure of his mouth. Almost reluctantly they drew away from each other.

'All right?' he asked quietly.

She nodded and her hand flew to her mouth to still its trembling. 'That shouldn't have happened,' she said unsteadily.

He inclined his head slightly. 'I agree . . . but don't worry about it. It isn't the first time a woman has become amorous under the influence of alcohol.' He spoke lightly, teasingly, in order to reassure her, very much shaken himself by that exchanged kiss, by the sweet enchantment he had found in that embrace. He fully appreciated how she must be feeling and he wanted to remove any embarrassment from the moment.

Vanessa stared at him, feeling the colour

ebb from her cheeks. 'Do you always oblige?' she asked with icicles dripping from the words. 'It must become rather monotonous for you—or perhaps it isn't too bad when you're a little under the influence yourself? I'm sorry I didn't give you time to have that drink.' She stalked past him and went into the house, leaving him bereft of words and conscious of a fierce anger that she should think his kiss had been so casual and meaningless.

He took out his cigarette case, smoked a cigarette before he returned to the party, and was in full control of himself by the time he entered the stuffy, noisy room. He looked for Vanessa almost instinctively. She was more animated than he had ever seen her, laughing and talking and flirting outrageously with the two men she had detached from Fiona's group of admirers.

He watched her for a few minutes, his anger growing, although he had believed it to be fully under control. It seemed to him that she was the one who treated a man's kiss as something casual and meaningless. It was impossible that she did not realise how much it had meant to him . . . how oddly it had affected him . . . how much he had longed to catch her to him again and seek to find that enchanted world once more. He had kissed many women in the course of his life—but it was the first time that the world had stood still for him, that his surroundings had taken on an unsuspected magic, that he had felt as though all the breath had been forced from his body and left him strangely breathless and light headed and aware of the blood stirring strongly in his veins.

She had invited his kiss. Heaven knew he had never been offered greater provocation than that uplifted face, that parted mouth and those sparkling eyes. He did not for a moment believe that the potent whisky was not to blame for her sweet and willing response to the pressure of his lips. That was understandable . . . but to dismiss the whole incident so casually, to behave as though he had insulted her and now to play up to those damned men so brazenly that his gall rose. Surely he was not mistaken in the wholesomeness and gentle reserve of Vanessa Clement. No, he could only blame the alcohol once more but nevertheless he meant to put a stop to her outrageous behaviour whether or not he had any right to do so.

He strode across the room. 'Vanessa!'

She looked at him coldly. 'That's my name.'

'You must be sober,' ragged one of her companions. 'One needs to be to remember which is which when the whole bevy of beauties are together.'

Justin withered him with a look. Then he turned to Vanessa. 'I want to talk to you.'

145

She was startled. But her anger against him was still fierce. 'I can't imagine that we have anything to say to each other.'

'I've plenty to say to you . . . when we're alone,' he said pointedly.

The same man shrugged. 'I guess we're *de trop*, Peter, old man,' he said to his friend . . . and they drifted away reluctantly.

Vanessa glared at Justin. 'How dared you barge in like that?'

'What the devil do you think you're doing?' he retorted grimly. He removed the glass from her hand and set it firmly on a nearby table. 'Keep off the drink—I won't be around to rescue you again.'

'You're not my keeper!' she flared. 'And I'll thank you to rescue someone else if you must be chivalrous—one such experience will serve me for a very long time.'

'I'll remember,' he assured her coldly. 'Believe me, I've better things to do than stand about in the cold night air keeping you on your feet. Take my advice . . . the next time you mix your drinks, make sure the nearest man is more appreciative of your amorous inclinations. I've never cared 'much for women who throw themselves at my head, sober or otherwise.'

Her eyes blazoned her fury. 'I think you'd better go,' she said shakily.

He nodded. 'Oh, I'm going . . . it sickens me to see a woman playing the tart. Or didn't

146

you realise that's what you were doing?'

'Have you quite finished?' She was perfectly calm now but her hands itched with the impulse to batter him insanely.

'I shall very soon be finished with the whole pack of you—and it will be quite a relief to get you off my back!' He turned on his heel and pushed his way through the mass of people to the door.

It was unlikely that his voice could have pierced the babble of sound but Vanessa felt as though everyone was looking in her direction, some curiously, some pityingly, some laughingly. How dared he say such things to her? How dared he be so offensive, so deliberately and damnably offensive?

Blindly she thrust her way through the crowd, stumbled down the steps and along the corridor to her room and threw herself in a torrent of tears on the bed.

She would never forgive him . . . never! He had flayed and humiliated her mercilessly before all those people. The contempt in his tone had been unmistakable . . . and the vile things he had said had completely destroyed the warm, tender, helpless love that she had been cherishing so foolishly. How could she have imagined herself in love with such a man? How could she ever have thought kindly of him when he had never granted them more than the barest courtesy and had shown his dislike and resentment so

147

blatantly? What manner of man was he to hate them all so much for something that they could not help . . . and which Vanessa, at least, had not wanted to happen?

He was despicable, loathsome, cruel . . . he was arrogant and presumptuous, self-centred and aggressive . . . he was intolerant and tyrannical . . . he was all the things she had believed him to be at that first meeting and then forgotten in that stupid fantasy of believing herself in love with him. She hated him . . . as much as he evidently hated her!

CHAPTER ELEVEN

Vanessa looked in each room of the flat for the last time, supposedly to check that nothing was forgotten, in reality needing a last look at the place where she had been so happy . . . and so miserable during the last few weeks. She could not feel that the new home would bring her either happiness or peace of mind.

Her suggestion that they should keep it on as a town flat had been vetoed by her sisters who scorned the place as shabby, too small, no longer in keeping with their new status and much too far from the bright lights and social life of the West End. Vanessa had dropped the subject. She no longer cared where she lived or what happened to her. Their plans, their arrangements, their suggestions and discussions seemed to have nothing to do with her—they merely slid over her wretchedness and indifference to what the future might bring. Her sisters assumed with some relief that she finally admitted the incredible wonder of their good fortune. They were far too wrapped up in their own plans and dreams to notice that she was ill with unhappiness. If she seemed a little strange, they charitably attributed it to shock and amazement and a foolish fear of the many changes in store for them all.

'Come on!' Belinda called impatiently, running up to drag her away. 'I don't know why you should be mooning about this place as though you can't bear to leave it. It isn't a patch on Fairlands—and what heaven to have a room to myself at last!'

Vanessa meekly followed her down to the waiting car. Her sisters were flushed and bright-eyed with excitement and chafing with impatience to be on their way. Fiona was driving herself in the sports car, the boot crammed with last-minute luggage. She had resolutely refused to take a passenger, declaring that any one of her sisters would drive her to distraction in their present state of mind. She was immaculately and beautifully dressed in the shocking pink suit with its white accessories and a silver fox fur thrown about her slim shoulders.

Because Belinda had not yet taken her driving test, her little coupé had been taken to Fairlands on the previous day by a friend and she was ill-pleased to be travelling in a hired car instead of arriving in similar style to Fiona.

With a gay wave of her hand and a promise to be at Fairlands to welcome them, Fiona put her foot on the accelerator and the elegant sports car shot away in a cloud of dust and disappeared around the corner.

Belinda sulked for the first ten minutes—then the excitement of Melissa and Rowena infected her own mood. Vanessa sat quietly in a corner and listened to the gay, trivial banter that passed between them. She realised perfectly well that they were puzzled by her silent withdrawal—and that they had long since lost patience with her dreary attitude to the entire affair. She could never hope for their understanding of her feelings—and so she kept them to herself and tried to struggle with her unhappiness.

She was dreading their arrival and the meeting with Justin. She was filled with a cold dread and a desperate embarrassment that was faintly tinged with the remnants of her anger against him. It was fortunate for her peace of mind that he would soon be leaving Fairlands. He had left her in no doubt as to his opinion of her on that dreadful

150

evening: she was still too wretched, too humiliated, to wonder at that cold and frightening anger in his eyes and voice.

Again and again she vehemently denied to herself that she did, in fact, love him despite that unprovoked attack. Again and again her treacherous heart brooked no denials. The love which had come so unexpectedly, so swiftly, had taken a firm hold of her heart and nothing, it seemed, could shake its depth, its sincerity, its insistent grip. She had been destined to love like this . . . hopelessly, helplessly . . . and she was very much afraid that no other man would ever be able to weaken the strength, the power and the need of that love. Incredible folly, perhaps . . . sheer stupidity, perhaps . . . insane awakening to a call that only she had heard, perhaps . . . but it was irrevocable and eternal and there was nothing she could do about it. Justin would walk out of her life very shortly . . . but she would go on loving him with an unalterable, unshakable love . . .

Fiona drove through the gates and along the wide, curving drive to the house, exulting in the beauty and magnificence that now belonged to them. Nothing and no one could take it away.

She had made good time on the journey and felt very pleased with herself and the performance of her car. It had been gratifying to know that she had caused a stir on the roads and in the quiet villages that she had passed through. All her life she had wanted to be a person who caused a stir: blessed with a vital beauty, a striking figure and a rich personality, all she had lacked was the necessary money. That lack had made little difference in the past for she had easily attracted the type of man who could afford expensive restaurants and nightclubs and moved on the fringe of society. But it was very nice to be wealthy . . . and she looked forward to causing even more of a stir once she took her place in the new society of which she was now a member.

At the sound of her voice in the hall, giving instructions to Madison in her cool, somewhat haughty manner, Clifford Gantry came out to greet her.

She was a little surprised, having expected Justin as the door opened, but she held out her hand with a warm smile. She had taken quite a fancy to the tall, rather austere bachelor with the greying temples and the kindly eyes. 'This is nice!' she exclaimed. 'Is this a social call or must we talk business so soon?'

He held her hand for a moment longer than was necessary. 'Justin has gone to Norfolk for a few days . . . he asked me to be here to welcome you in his place,' he explained.

She raised an amused eyebrow. 'Very thoughtful of him. Well, I'd much rather be welcomed by you than Justin. I'm afraid his grimness would be too much of a damper on this day of all days.'

He was slightly taken aback. 'You find him grim?'

She wrinkled her nose prettily. 'Well, we're not on the best of terms, you know. I imagine he would be a different man if he would only relax and accept the inevitable.'

'He always speaks of you all quite warmly,' he said firmly. Justin had never hinted at any feud between the Clements and himself . . . and he was vaguely disappointed by the hardness of Fiona's tone and the contemptuous shrug of her shoulders when she talked of him.

Fiona strolled into the drawing-room, loosening the fur from her shoulders and throwing it carelessly across a chair. 'Would you like a drink—or do you prefer coffee at this time of the day?'

'Coffee, I think.'

She moved to the fireplace to press the bell, looking about the room with faint distaste. It was a pity that Piers and Nigel were so busy at the moment that her plans to improve Fairlands had to wait for the time being. The room was really very shabby . . . 'You have a place near us, don't you, Mr. Gantry?' she asked politely.

'About five miles away,' he agreed. He smiled at her across the room. 'Couldn't you make it Cliff, by the way?'

She picked up a cigarette box and offered it to him. 'Of course—if you'll make it Fiona,' she returned lightly, her eyes dancing. Perhaps he was not such a confirmed bachelor nor so austere as he had seemed at first. She rather thought that she would appreciate this man's interest and friendship.

'When are your sisters due to arrive?' he asked, as though he was a little uncertain of his ground as their eyes met.

'They should be here quite soon. We left together but my Sprite knows how to eat up the miles. I love fast cars, don't you?' Madison came into the room and she broke off to order coffee. As he went out with his ponderous tread, she smiled up at Cliff from the comfortable settee. 'Do sit down . . . So Justin's gone to Norfolk. About this job with Lord Stokes, I suppose?'

'Yes, I believe so.' He was very conscious of the faint, delicate perfume she wore, of the perfectly lovely curve of her cheekbone and the shining mass of her dark hair in its sophisticated dressing.

'He mentioned it to Vanessa.' She studied the tip of her cigarette thoughtfully. 'I hope you haven't the impression that we want him to go, Cliff. It was his own decision.'

'So he told me. I think he would have found it rather difficult to stay at Fairlands in the circumstances—it was a great blow to him when his uncle died so suddenly and without leaving a will.'

Fiona flicked ash from her cigarette. 'We're very sorry for him, of course . . .'

'He wouldn't want that,' Cliff interposed swiftly. 'He's a very proud man, Fiona.'

'Well, we do appreciate how he feels and his decision to go is quite understandable. But I should be sorry if he was going merely because we haven't been able to get on with him. It's really been very difficult—he hasn't made any attempt to conceal his resentment of us.'

He frowned. 'I'm surprised to hear it. I've always found Justin very easy and good-natured.'

'But you haven't taken Fairlands from him!'

'Do you really think he bears you a grudge for that? I'm sure you must be mistaken. Justin is really very shy at heart and it takes him some time to feel at ease with people he doesn't know.'

Privately Fiona thought that they could not be discussing the same man. But she wisely did not say so. 'Well, he certainly hasn't been very friendly,' she said emphatically. 'And it never occurred to any of us that he might be shy!'

He looked at her steadily, as though he sensed her unspoken thought. 'It's odd that different people can see the same man in a different light,' he said with a wry smile.

She touched his hand briefly. 'I know he's your friend, Cliff . . . I'm sorry if I've offended you by being so blunt. But I wish I could convince you that he's managed to make us feel like impostors!'

'It's been difficult for all of you to adjust,' he said mildly. 'I expect things won't be too easy for you and your sisters at first . . . please call on me at any time. I shall be glad to advise you and do what I can to help you.'

'Thank you,' she said warmly. 'I'll warn you now that I shall take every advantage of that offer, my dear.'

'I hope you will,' he replied quietly and with unmistakable meaning.

Fiona met the kindly, sincere gaze of his grey eyes and a strangely welcome warmth stole into her veins. She liked him immensely. He was very different to the men who usually attracted her with his quiet reserve and oddly appealing formality but she felt that she could trust him implicitly and that he would prove to be a reliable and valuable friend. It was very pleasant to have these few minutes with him . . . heartwarming to realise that he liked and admired her in return. Was it possible that she was seriously attracted to this man—certainly she had been aware of swift delight at his presence in the house and she did not resent the gentle rebukes she had sensed in his comments about their dealings with Justin. It might be very welcome to place her life in the responsible and kindly care of Clifford Gantry—but there was time enough to talk of marriage when a firm friendship had been cemented . . .

Vanessa steeled herself to meet Justin—quite unnecessarily as she learned within a few minutes of their arrival. Yet far from being relieved, she knew a bitter disappointment. Even his antagonism was preferable to his absence!

As she unpacked and renewed the ravages of the journey, she tried to think of her new, oddly unwelcoming surroundings as home. Naturally they would need a few days to settle in but Vanessa wondered if Fairlands would ever seem a home to her. Perhaps if Justin were to stay, if time could erase the antagonism and bring about some measure of friendship between them, if she could really adapt herself to the strange, new way of life . . . But Justin was probably in Norfolk finalising his plans for the future and it was unlikely that he would want to keep in touch with them. And Vanessa did not feel that she could ever adapt to the life that her sisters had embraced so eagerly.

The sound of a car through the open window sent her flying from her room and down the stairs in the foolish hope that Justin had returned earlier than expected. She did not pause to wonder what he might think of her haste, her flushed cheeks and suspiciously bright eyes.

She checked her eager flight and finished the descent slowly as Morny and Raif Fitzgerald were admitted by the impeccable Madison. She went forward to greet them and the butler discreetly withdrew to the staff quarters. Vanessa was not sure what the staff thought of their inheritance of Fairlands . . . but they had all agreed to stay with the Clements at Justin's request.

'Are we your first visitors?' Morny demanded gaily.

Vanessa smiled. 'Not quite . . . Mr. Gantry is here.'

'Yes, of course. Justin told me he'd asked him to be here. Raif and I are on our way to look at a mare for Father but we couldn't pass without calling to see if you'd arrived.' She threw her brother an impish look as she spoke which puzzled Vanessa a little. Raif merely smiled.

'Is it too early to offer you a drink?' Vanessa asked hesitantly.

Raif grinned. 'It's never too early to offer . . . but, no thanks, not for me. I don't know about this reprobate sister of mine.'

Morny ignored his remark scornfully. 'Where is everybody?' she asked as they went into the empty drawing-room.

'I really don't know.' Vanessa frowned.

158

'Fiona was in here with Mr. Gantry a little while ago. The others are in their rooms but I expect they'll be down soon.'

Even as she spoke, Melissa entered the room . . . but she paused uncertainly on the threshold as she saw the Fitzgeralds.

Raif smiled at her encouragingly. She was such a shy little thing, he thought tenderly . . . strangely in contrast to the self-assured Fiona. 'Well, how does it feel to be in possession?' he teased.

Melissa looked uncomfortable. 'I don't know yet.'

'Oh, Melissa would be happy anywhere as long as she was near a piano,' Vanessa said lightly and turned to Morny to reply to a question.

Raif walked over to the magnificent piano. 'Is this the Waltheimer?' he asked. He raised the lid and touched the keys almost reverently. 'Come and try it, Melissa,' he invited. 'I can only manage Chopsticks and that would seem rather out of keeping with this edifice.'

She joined him and fingered the keys uncertainly. He was so handsome, so nice—and she felt so stupidly young, so unsure of herself, so shy whenever she saw him. He treated her with an easy, natural friendliness . . . only Fiona knew the ardent looks, the meaning pressure of his hand, the murmured endearments. It was really not fair, Melissa thought resentfully—Fiona could take her pick from a dozen men . . . why did she encourage Raif when she openly admitted that, charming though he might be, she thought him somewhat immature and irresponsible. He had no such faults in Melissa's eyes. But he was only interested in Fiona and it came easily to him to behave as though any woman he was with was the only one in the world. Justin had said he was an incorrigible flirt . . . perhaps that was true but Melissa never felt that he was flirting with her. It was unthinkable that he might ever consider her company and her stilted, naive conversation preferable to Fiona's vivacity and beauty and easy manners. But there was no law against wishing—and in that moment she wished with all her heart that she might not learn to love Raif Fitzgerald. It would be very easy to love him—and that would be a sheer waste of emotion.

'Play something,' he suggested quietly.

She shook her head. 'Not now . . . the others are talking—and besides, Fiona will come in soon.' She looked up at him shyly. 'She and Mr. Gantry have only gone to look over the farm.'

Raif raised an incredulous eyebrow. 'I didn't know Fiona was interested in farming.'

'Mr. Gantry was explaining about the income from the farm and telling us about the new lambs—and Fiona decided that she'd like

160

to see them.'

'I see . . . and you're not interested in lambs?'

'Oh yes! But Mr. Gantry seemed to want to be alone with Fiona . . .' She broke off abruptly, wondering if she had been tactless.

'Did he, indeed? Good for him! I thought he was immune to feminine charms,' he said lightly. 'But he might have chosen someone a little less complicated than Fiona for his first taste of romance, though.' He grinned. 'She'll have him dancing to her tune and liking it in no time.'

Melissa's eyes widened at the faint malice of his tone. 'Don't you like Fiona?'

'Adore her,' he retorted carelessly. 'She's a remarkably attractive woman. But a bit too haughty for me—and much too temperamental. I like to know where I am with a woman.' He glanced at her bewildered face. 'Good heavens! Did you imagine I was in love with Fiona?' he exclaimed with sudden perception.

'Yes, of course,' she returned unsteadily, her heart leaping with foolish new hope.

'Silly infant,' he said indulgently. But he did not add that he had realised the emptiness of his infatuation for Fiona on the night of the party—not that he had abruptly realised the shy sweetness and fair loveliness of her younger sister and that he had persuaded Morny to call at Fairlands that morning

161

because he wanted to see Melissa again, wanted to discover if the strange emotion she had stirred to life had survived once the enchantment of the evening was at an end. He had never felt for any woman this tender desire to protect and cherish, this deep-rooted conviction that the only happiness the future held for him was to be found in Melissa's sweetness and shy warmth.

He had told himself that he must tread warily and slowly, employing patience and kindness and tenderness to win Melissa rather than the impetuous, passionate approach to a short-lived affair that had won him a reputation as a womaniser.

But now, looking into those grey eyes, so warm with obvious relief, he wondered with a leaping heart if the goal was nearer than he thought, if she was on the verge of loving him already . . .

CHAPTER TWELVE

The sisters were in the drawing-room with their coffee after dinner when Justin returned, walking in unexpectedly, pulling off his leather driving gloves. His hair was slightly ruffled and his expression was faintly weary after the long drive from Norfolk.

Vanessa sunk deeper into her chair,

162

wishing she could disappear altogether. The grimness of his expression, the lack of warmth in his perfunctory smile, the curtness of his general greeting was not encouraging. She could imagine his feelings at finding them all so much at home—and she regretted that their ill-concealed surprise must make him feel like an unwanted intruder.

Fiona was coolly composed. 'Good evening. Did you have a good journey? Belinda, ring the bell—we'll need another cup. Have you eaten, Justin?'

'I had dinner on the road, thanks.' His mouth tightened at her gracious air of playing hostess . . . damn her, this had been his home for as long as he could remember and he was quite capable of informing Madison of his needs if any. 'Don't bother about coffee for me,' he said curtly. 'I'm going to change right now.' And he spun on his heel and walked from the room.

Fiona shrugged. 'He's determined not to unbend,' she commented impatiently.

'I don't know why you bother about him,' Belinda retorted. 'He's so damned surly I feel that I never want to speak to him again.'

'I expect he's tired,' Vanessa defended swiftly.

'Oh, you're always making excuses for him. You might as well save your breath, Van—he won't thank you for flying to his defence.' Belinda returned to her magazine.

'We have to live with him for the time being,' Vanessa said quietly. 'What's the point of being at loggerheads all the time?'

'Well, I tried to be pleasant,' Fiona reminded her.

'You might have been less condescending about it,' Vanessa snapped. Suddenly the company of her sisters was intolerable. She leaped to her feet and hurried from the room.

Oh, she hated this house! She hated the changes that money had brought. It seemed she could not be five minutes in the same room as her sisters without being involved in a difference of opinion. Oh, to turn back the clock to those halcyon days of comparative poverty when everything had been so different!

She was halfway up the wide staircase when Justin came out of his room and strode resolutely to the head of the stairs. He saw her and paused . . . for a long moment they looked at each other. Then, catching at her composure, tilting her chin swiftly in a gesture of hauteur, Vanessa carried on to the top of the stairs. He stepped aside for her to pass. Vanessa swept on without a word or a glance for there had been something in his expression, a certain narrowed assessment, that had infuriated her.

Justin involuntarily put a hand on her arm. 'Have you nothing to say to me?' he asked in unconscious resentment.

She stiffened. How dared he use that tone to her! Did he expect her to indulge in idle chit-chat with him after all that had passed between them at their last meeting . . . and when he had completely ignored her only a few minutes ago? 'I can't imagine that we have anything to say to each other,' she said coldly. 'Unless you wish to apologise.' She looked down at his restraining hand so pointedly that he released her immediately.

'For kissing you? I'm damned if I will!' he retorted angrily. 'Where's the offence in kissing a willing woman?'

Vanessa felt the hot colour rush to her cheeks. If only she was in a position to deny her willingness . . . but he had sensed the response in her body and lips to his embrace and it would be foolish to argue the point.

'How despicable you are!' she exclaimed in low but effective tones.

He looked down at her . . . then with a sudden, impatient movement he turned away and ran briskly down the stairs. He derided himself for having paused to speak to her—she was determined to maintain the ill-feeling that existed between them. It would be pointless to attempt the offer of an olive-branch and he would not go out of his way to speak to her again.

Justin wished that the memory of their last meeting would not torment him so much. He had lost his temper—and regretted it. He had said wild, meaningless, angry things—and she would not forgive him. It was true that he should apologise . . . he had deliberately misunderstood her—but he was a proud and rebellious man and he would not abase himself at any woman's bidding. He had been ready to apologise, he had paused for that very reason, delighting in her fair loveliness as she approached him and knowing that he wanted and needed her liking and friendship and wished an end to their hostility. But she had been so cold, so haughty, so remote that the words had died on his lips—and the impulse had died with equal rapidity at her prompting.

Let her hug her wounded feelings! Let them remain enemies for the short time that remained before he left Fairlands for ever!

He admitted her right to an apology. He had lost his temper over a stupid, trifling incident—egotistical of him to imagine that his kiss could mean anything to a woman who had shown her dislike of him often enough. What on earth had she thought of his insane outburst? She had been furious—that was evident. She had been completely bewildered by it—that was understandable. He had irrevocably put himself beyond the pale as far as she was concerned. Why should it matter so much? She was a Clement—tarred with the same brush as her conceited, wilful, arrogant sisters who had taken to money like ducks to water. He despised the whole pack of them and he was determined to put them all out of his mind when he left Fairlands and immerse himself in the work that was waiting for him.

He went into his study and slammed the door. But he could not slam the door so easily on his thoughts and his disturbed emotions. It would not be so easy to forget Vanessa . . . the memory of her slim, soft body, her warm and eager lips, the sweet scent of her hair and the feel of her arms about his neck was deeply etched on his mind and heart . . .

Vanessa went into her room and closed the door quietly, her heart pounding and leaping like a wild thing—and an inconsolable sorrow stirring in her blood. He had been so cold, so resentful, so aloof . . . impossible to reach a man like that who showed so plainly that he despised and distrusted her.

She went to the window and looked over the twilit gardens, feeling utterly wretched. She wished she had not goaded him about an apology . . . she would prefer the entire incident forgotten and it had been stupid to mention it.

Oh, Justin, she mourned silently, couldn't you have spoken one friendly word, one kind greeting? Couldn't you have given me the merest hint of a smile? Do you hate me so much? Is it so unbearable to be under the same roof with me?

She wished she could forget his kiss, the

strength of his arms about her, the tenderness of his embrace—for it had meant nothing. She might have been any woman offering her lips casually, carelessly, fleetingly. But she knew she would never forget the sweet, thrilling wonder of his lips on her own and she hungered again for their touch.

If only she could banish her love for him, think of him as coldly and harshly as he thought of her, ignore the impact he had made on her life and her heart. Soon, much too soon, he would be gone without a backward glance or a twinge of regret—and her life would be bleak and empty and hopeless . . .

During the days that followed, Justin came into little contact with the Clements. By design, he was extremely busy and there was plenty to do in showing John Byfield the ropes, working with him on the estate accounts, advising and suggesting and teaching. He spent his few hours of freedom from work with Morny and he found her company easeful, relaxing and comforting after the cold, continued antagonism of the Clements.

Morny could not understand his dislike of the newcomers and said as much. For herself, she had found them friendly and pleasant and easy to like . . . and her brother was frequently at Fairlands.

Justin smiled faintly. 'Yes, I know . . . I'm

always falling over him,' he retorted lightly.

'Raif likes them all. But he's really bowled over this time, Justin.' She frowned slightly. 'I know Fiona is lovely and charming and I really do like her—but I don't know that I'd care for her as a sister-in-law.'

'No fear of that,' he told her easily. 'Melissa draws him to Fairlands, my dear—not Fiona.'

Her eyes widened. 'Melissa! That shy little mouse! You can't be serious!'

Justin shrugged. 'That's how it looks to me. He flirts with Fiona . . . but Melissa is the one he talks to seriously and tries to coax out of her shyness. Why should he bother if he isn't half in love with her? As you say, she's a shy little thing . . . I've barely exchanged half a dozen words with her since they've been at Fairlands.'

'That isn't really surprising, is it?' she asked bluntly. 'I doubt if you've exchanged half a dozen words with any of them from what I hear. Why, you never meet them except for meals . . . and even then you're often late or are too busy to have anything more than a snatched sandwich and cup of coffee in the study.'

Justin laughed lightly. 'You really are *au fait* with the situation, aren't you?'

'What is it between you and the Clements?' she persisted. 'I can't believe you resent them so much because they have Fairlands.'

He shrugged. 'Call it mutual dislike. They want to see the back of me as soon as possible—and I won't be sorry to bid them farewell.'

'You've changed,' she told him bluntly. 'You're hard and cold and bitter . . . and it's only since the Clements took over Fairlands. What's wrong, Justin? I'm sure you could be friends if you would. But you're scathing about Fiona, contemptuous of the others—and you never mention Vanessa's name, to my knowledge.' She glanced at him curiously.

She had her suspicions about his reserve where Vanessa Clement was concerned—and although it hurt a little to know that she had lost him, she would rather his happiness was assured. She was not and never had been really in love with Justin but she was very attached to him and the dream of marrying him one day had been a pleasant and often-indulged habit. Lately she had realised that his unusually affectionate manner was not evoked by any warmer feeling on his part but more as a protest against an emotion some other woman had kindled. That woman, Morny knew with feminine intuition, was Vanessa.

She went on easily, hoping to invite his confidence: 'Vanessa's the best of the bunch, I think. She's really a very sweet person. I wish she was happier at Fairlands—but, of course, you may not have noticed as you don't see much of her. I'm sure she feels terrible about the whole business.'

'Nonsense!' He spoke curtly and Morny knew she had made a mistake. 'Like her sisters, Vanessa behaves as though she owns Fairlands . . . and as though I were the outsider and the usurper.'

He made his way back to Fairlands, Morny's words echoing in his thoughts. Why the devil should Vanessa be unhappy? She had everything she wanted . . . and much she cared for his feelings in the matter of Fairlands or anything else.

He passed John Byfield and Rowena, hands linked, heads close together as they walked and talked with the air of two young people who had forgotten the world around them. He smiled faintly. Byfield had wasted no time in attaching himself to Rowena and she was evidently not averse to the attentions of a paid employee of the estate. He wondered idly if this swift, youthful infatuation would develop into something more in time . . . and then remembered that he would not be around to watch its development.

The pale blue coupé was standing outside the house and as he parked his car behind it, Belinda and Vanessa came out. He glanced at Vanessa. There were violet shadows beneath her eyes that even her cleverly-applied make-up could not conceal—indication that she was not sleeping well or that she was as unhappy at Fairlands as Morny had claimed. Well, she was not losing sleep over him, he thought grimly, remembering the nights when he had tossed and turned in an agony of longing and slept only to dream wild, impossible dreams of Vanessa.

Love and its acknowledgment had not come easily to him. He had denied its unwelcome stirrings for as long as he could. There were a thousand women in the world who would possibly welcome his love and respond to it gladly. So what had possessed him to fall in love with a woman who avoided him as much as she could, obviously disliked him and would no more think of loving him than the man in the moon!

Yet, as his heart stirred with sudden warmth at the sight of those dark shadows and the pale, unhappy face, he could no longer deny the irrevocable truth. He loved Vanessa, would give anything to win her friendship and liking, deeply regretted all that had passed between them and wished there were some way to break through the icy barrier of pride and hostility that she presented to him whenever they chanced to meet.

For a brief moment of time, he had believed that she loved him. Her response to his kiss had been so sweet, so trusting, so whole-hearted, every fibre of her being

172

seemingly attuned to the tumultuous pounding of a new and exciting emotion in his own being. Then she had scorned the feeling that all her feminine perception must have sensed . . . and in his pain and anger he had tried to hurt her in return with wild, senseless words.

During his stay in Norfolk, he had told himself that he had frightened her with too swift a revelation of the way he felt about her, that she was shy of the strange emotion kindled between them. He had thought often and long of their next meeting . . . of how he would speak to her, how their eyes would meet in wordless communication, how each would know in that moment that all was well between them and that their love was mutual and eternal and allowing of only one result . . . their eventual marriage.

But that meeting had shattered his dream. There had been no leaping light of welcome, no warm word of greeting, nothing but a cold indifference which had deeply wounded him. He was both proud and sensitive and it had never been easy for him to reveal his innermost feelings to anyone . . . so he had concealed them behind a veneer of angry resentment and antagonism which only made matters very much worse.

He stepped out of his car and walked towards the steps. Belinda threw him a haughty glance and would have turned to her car without a word for him. But Vanessa's hand on her arm checked her swiftly. She could not ignore him as though he did not exist although there was every likelihood that he would return a snub to any remark she made to him.

She managed to smile tremulously—but it would have been easier to succumb to the tears that smarted suddenly as she met his cool, questioning eyes. 'Hallo . . . we're just going to Town. Is there anything we can bring back for you?' She was angry with herself for the shy, embarrassed awkwardness of her question.

'No, I don't think so. I'm going to Town myself at the weekend, thanks.' He paused briefly, knowing he had sounded curt and ungracious, seeking the right words to make amends. 'It's a lovely day for the drive,' he said, as callow as any young boy with love in his heart and the clamp of shyness on his tongue when faced with the only woman in the world who mattered.

'Yes, it is,' Belinda said pertly. 'It would be a shame to delay it any longer.' She had no time at all for Justin Fairgarth and did not hesitate to let him know it.

Vanessa's swift glance held a rebuke for the unnecessary discourtesy. After all, it had been a natural remark to make and his tone had been pleasant enough.

They had been avoiding each other

successfully for days. It seemed a pity to snub him on the only occasion that he had gone out of his way to speak to her. Perhaps if she was pleasant in return, if she showed him a little friendly warmth, it might not be too late to salvage something from the debris of their association. She could not bear much more of this antagonism between them. Every morning, after a restless, disturbed night, she woke to the miserable certainty that Justin would be as distant and unfriendly as on the day before and that the incessant ache of her heart would still be denied the ease of a moment's kindness, a fleeting smile, the merest warmth in his eyes.

It was not easy to face him without a familiar rush of remembered humiliation. Once his eyes had held hers with so much tenderness in their depths; once his arms had held her close to his heart with so much passion; once she had known the fierce, wonderful sweetness of his kiss. Those memories were very vivid even if they were overshadowed by the memory of his anger and contempt, things which she had surely not merited and completely failed to understand. If only she knew what she had done or said to offend this proud, difficult man. But she had never dared to ask and he had offered neither explanation nor apology.

'It's too nice a day for you to spend it in working,' she said impulsively. 'Why don't you come with us?'

'Vanessa!' Belinda exclaimed reproachfully. 'You must be awfully naive if you don't know by now that Mr. Fairgarth can't bear to breathe the same air as a Clement.'

Vanessa flushed and Justin knew a surge of anger against her sister for causing the woman he loved that moment of embarrassment. 'Spare us the dramatic heights,' he said curtly. 'I've no intention of spoiling your day by accepting the invitation. My work is important.' He nodded to Vanessa, scarcely realising that his anger was very evident in his eyes, unconscious of the dismay and pain that his curt comment brought in its wake. 'Thanks . . . but you don't have to worry about me,' he told her, almost brusquely.

'You make it very difficult for people to like you!' she flared out of her pain. 'No wonder Fairlands has such a hostile atmosphere—you infect it with your antagonism to us!'

'Well, you won't have to endure my presence much longer,' he said harshly and left them abruptly.

'I don't know why you bother with him,' Belinda said crossly as Vanessa stumbled blindly into the car. 'He's a most objectionable man! Anyone would think you were in love with him!' she turned to grin impishly. 'You're not, I suppose?'

'Don't talk nonsense—and let's get moving

if we're going to Town,' she retorted sharply, angrily.

Belinda's eyes widened. 'You can't love him!' she exclaimed furiously. 'Oh, how can you even like him, Van?'

'Concentrate on the road,' Vanessa told her fiercely as the small car shot through the gates and into the main road, narrowly missing a cyclist.

'No wonder you invited him to come with us! Haven't you any pride? He treats you like dirt—and yet you still run after him. You won't get anywhere with a man that way!'

'I appreciate the benefit of your wide experience,' Vanessa said with heavy sarcasm. 'But your advice is quite unnecessary. I'm not even interested in Justin Fairgarth—certainly I'm not likely to fall in love with him.' It was not a lie, she comforted herself hastily—it was much too late to consider falling in love. She had tumbled helplessly and hopelessly into love long ago . . .

CHAPTER THIRTEEN

Belinda had a hair appointment and Vanessa had accepted her offer of a lift to Town in order to do some shopping. They lunched and then the sisters parted on the arrangement to meet at the same restaurant for coffee at four-thirty.

Vanessa walked along Regent Street, idly glancing in shop windows, her thoughts far from the new clothes she needed. She had managed to dress well enough to please her sisters without touching a penny of her newly-acquired income, drawing on the money she had saved in the past. She still felt that she was not entitled to live in luxury on money that should belong to Justin but she supposed that in time she would use it as carelessly and easily as her sisters.

If only everything had been different, she thought sadly. As she walked, heedless of the traffic, the passers-by, the fashionable shops, she idly dwelt on the pleasing fancy that Justin had inherited Fairlands, as seemed right and natural, that he had learned of the existence of his cousins and sought them out of curiosity, that there had been immediate, mutual liking and respect and that he had then proceeded to fall in love with Vanessa as swiftly as she had fallen in love with him!

She could be happy at Fairlands as Justin's wife—but never in the role of hated usurper. It was a relief to escape from its oppressive hostility for a few hours—and it was almost bliss to feel free of the possibility that she would encounter Justin and have to suffer the renewed awareness of his dislike. What *had* she done to incur so much enmity? She had been friendly, pleasant, willing to accept him as a cousin at the beginning. She had stupidly mixed her drinks at that beastly party and allowed—no, she amended honestly . . . *encouraged* him to kiss her. She had justifiably flared at him when he sneered at the passionate response she had shown—and then he had dragged her away from friends and insulted her beyond bearing. It was so ridiculous! He was not even supposed to be at the party . . . had turned up without warning at a late hour and had left almost as precipitately as he had arrived. Had he only gone to find an opportunity to humiliate her? That was how it seemed . . . but with what motive—and why her in particular? She had been so deceived by that pretence of warmth and concern. He had *wanted* to kiss her . . . nothing could shake that conviction although he had implied that her alcoholic desires were entirely to blame for that brief interlude under the stars.

Since that night, she had tried to avoid him—at every unavoidable encounter they had bandied harsh, angry words. In so short a time, he would be gone—and she could not even hope for one friendly word, one hint of regret before he walked out of her life.

If only he had never walked into it that day. If only they were still living at the flat, content with their ordinary, normal way of life, happy in their affection for each other. She missed the flat with its atmosphere of warm homeliness and welcoming cheer. Filled with sudden nostalgia for its familiar rooms, she hailed a taxi quite impulsively and gave the driver the address.

She leaned forward in her seat, scanning the familiar streets, recognising well-known landmarks which had always told her that she was nearing home. They arrived and she paid off the taxi and stood outside the big house, looking up at the windows with wistful eyes. This was her home, she thought resentfully—not the big, hostile house where she had lived during recent weeks.

But now someone else lived here, someone else loved and laughed in the comfortable rooms, someone else cared for its cleanliness and comfort. She knew that Belinda had recommended some friends to take over the flat and now she wondered if she knew the people. They might give her some tea and allow her to look over the flat, so rich with memories. She mounted the steps and rang the bell . . . and then changed her mind. She turned away and began to hurry down the steps . . . but she was too late. The door opened and a familiar voice exclaimed her name.

Vanessa spun round. 'Belinda!'

'What on earth are you doing here?' her sister demanded petulantly. 'Did you follow me?'

'Follow you?' she echoed blankly. She

managed to smile. 'Did you feel nostalgic, too?' she asked lightly yet feeling a wave of affinity with her younger sister for the first time in weeks.

'I suppose you'd better come in,' Belinda returned brusquely and without any welcoming warmth in her tone.

'Who is it, darling?' a man's voice called.

'One of my sisters,' she called back ungraciously.

'Oh, damn!' he said with unmistakable annoyance.

Vanessa hesitated. 'Look . . . I don't want to intrude, Belinda.'

'Don't be silly.' Belinda smiled suddenly, her sulkiness banished. 'Come up and meet Guy . . . you might as well be introduced to your future brother-in-law.'

Vanessa stared in amazement. 'You're engaged? But when . . . to whom . . . how . . . ?'

Belinda urged her towards the stairs. 'Just now . . . to Guy Benjamin . . . and surely it doesn't need much explanation, Van. We're in love and we want to be married—that's how.'

Vanessa turned to face her. 'Not *the* Benjamin—that tyrannical, pigheaded, conceited old devil who always told you what a terrible actress you are!' she exclaimed, laughing gaily. 'Oh, Belinda, what a turncoat you've turned out to be!'

'Ssh . . . he'll hear you!' she said furiously.

Guy Benjamin leaned over the rail to tweak her hair. 'I heard every word . . . and it doesn't surprise me, my sweet. You told me what you thought of me a dozen times during rehearsals.' He straightened as Vanessa reached him and held out his hand. 'So you're one of the sisters—which one?' he asked easily.

'It's Vanessa,' Belinda said hastily.

He nodded. 'Ah, yes . . . I remember. Not the eldest, are you? I don't have to bend the knee before you and beseech Belinda's hand in marriage?'

Vanessa chuckled. She liked this tall, charming Irishman on sight—and her heart was full of happiness for Belinda as she saw the loving, tender glance that they briefly exchanged. 'No, that's Fiona. I merely give my blessing . . . and my warmest congratulations.'

'Is it a matter for congratulations?' he riposted. 'To be plagued in my old age by a sweet-tongued little wench who thinks I'll use my influence to get her to the West End.'

Vanessa smiled at him. 'And will you?'

'No,' he said bluntly. 'I'll use my belt to keep her in the kitchen where women belong . . . but she can keep her illusions till we're wed. Come and have a drink, sister—the foulest whisky that ever passed my lips but it serves the purpose.' He went before them

182

into the sitting-room and Vanessa paused to speak to her sister.

'But why didn't you tell me that you were meeting him? Why the fictitious hair appointment?'

Belinda shrugged. 'I knew you'd disapprove and do the elder-sister act. But I don't care whether you like Guy or not . . . I'm going to marry him and that's all there is to it.'

'I do like him,' Vanessa assured her. 'Why wouldn't I—I think he's charming.'

'He's been married before . . . and he's nearly twenty years older than I am,' Belinda said honestly.

Vanessa smiled. 'Does that worry you?'

'Not in the least,' she returned firmly and with obvious truth.

Vanessa kissed her cheek impulsively. 'Then you should be very happy.'

'Come along, women . . . don't whisper secrets behind my back!' Guy Benjamin bellowed loudly. 'The quality of the whisky won't improve for standing . . . Belinda, my sweet, in heaven's name—why Scotch whisky? Tis poison to a palate weaned on the best Irish liquor.'

'I always threatened to poison you one day,' she retorted pertly.

Vanessa enjoyed that afternoon immensely. For those few careless, wildly amusing hours, she could forget Justin, Fairlands, everything that troubled her so much and made her feel so wretched. She could not drink the whisky that Guy offered . . . it was too forcible a reminder of that party night when she had unwisely and unthinkingly drained the whisky from someone else's glass. He had not insisted, merely applauding her common-sense and good taste—and then he had rummaged in the kitchen cupboards till he found a bottle of cooking sherry which she had accepted laughingly and found quite tolerable enough to drink a toast to their happiness in it. If Guy and Belinda resented her intrusion at such a time, it was not obvious . . . and she was delighted to see how neatly and adroitly Guy handled her somewhat difficult sister. She had no fears for Belinda's future—and she resolutely stifled the stirring of envy and anxiety as to her own future.

Belinda and Vanessa drove back to Fairlands at a much later hour than they had intended. Belinda was silent for the most part as they drove through the countryside and Vanessa left her to her thoughts. Any woman who did not know and understand the demands of the theatre might have resented the fact that she could not be with the man she loved on the night of their engagement. Guy had suggested that they should watch the production but Belinda had teasingly retorted that she would be tempted to leap on the stage and show her replacement exactly how to play the part.

They drove on through the deepening dusk of the evening. Suddenly, Belinda slowed the car as the bright, beckoning lights of a roadhouse leaped to meet them.

'Lord, I'm hungry!' she exclaimed. 'And we'll be too late for dinner. Let's stop here and have a meal.'

Vanessa agreed for it was a long time since lunch and Guy had only been able to provide a sandwich and some biscuits, explaining that he would have a meal after the performance and that he rarely bothered to cook for himself. At the moment, he was sharing the flat with a friend, a television actor who had been rehearsing all day for a new show. But when Belinda and Guy were married, they would live at the flat and decorate and furnish it lavishly. Listening to their eager plans, Vanessa had been faintly surprised by her sister's readiness to fall in with this scheme and she wondered if she was not the only one to have been unhappy at Fairlands and to feel nostalgic for the old days at the flat. Belinda had seemed happy, seemed to enjoy the luxury and comfort of the new way of life but she had always been resilient and adaptable. No doubt she would adapt with equal ease to being the wife of a theatrical producer with all the demands made on him. It was obvious that Belinda was ambitious for him, that she did not expect him to stay at the Little Theatre for ever.

They lingered over the meal for Belinda was overflowing with excitement and her plans for the future—and Vanessa was content to listen and observe her undoubted radiant happiness.

It did not occur to either of them that their lateness might be causing any anxiety . . . but even while they ate and drank and talked, absorbed in the events of the day, Fiona was explaining to Justin Fairgarth that she had certainly expected them back to dinner and indeed earlier.

'I should think they decided to stay in Town . . . probably met some friends,' he said carelessly.

'Without telephoning?' she retorted scornfully. 'Then you don't know Vanessa! She'd never let me worry like this . . . I'm sure there's been an accident. That wretched car! And Belinda's so reckless . . . perhaps you haven't allowed her to drive you anywhere? I have! She's much too empty-headed to concentrate on the road when she's driving. She must always be babbling on and looking at anything that catches her eye.'

'I'm sure you're worrying quite needlessly,' he assured her but her anxiety had communicated itself to him and his eyes darkened as he thought of Vanessa, involved in an accident, in pain or stranded in a quiet country lane with a badly hurt Belinda on her hands, both of them possibly dead . . . A faint shudder passed through him. Hastily he thrust a mental door on the agonising picture that had come to him in that moment. 'If there had been an accident of any kind, we would have known by now, Fiona.' His voice held kindness, understanding and warmth for her fear and distress were evident. If it was true that Vanessa was much too thoughtful to alter her plans without letting her sister know then her anxiety was quite understandable. He realised abruptly how little he really knew of Vanessa, how little chance he had had to get to know her, how foolish it had been to carry on a childish vendetta when they could have been cementing a friendship. All for the sake of pride and a ridiculous determination that he would not apologise, would not unbend, would not be the first to ease the situation.

Fiona ran her hand through her dark hair, careless that she ruined its sophisticated styling. 'Oh, its silly to worry like this,' she admitted with some agitation. 'But Vanessa is always so considerate. Belinda wouldn't think of telephoning, I know—it never occurs to her that anyone might worry about her. She's always claiming that she can look after herself.'

'Why not telephone some of your friends

and find out if they've seen anything of your sisters?' he suggested. 'They might have mentioned their plans for the evening.' He realised that she needed to be doing something, however abortive it might prove to be. He had not known that such a depth of feeling existed between the sisters . . . for the short time that he had known them, they had seemed far from close, completely selfish and absorbed in their own plans, frequently bickering over trifles and not at all demonstrative. Now he realised that a strong bond of affection held them together despite outward appearances and that Fiona really did take her role as elder sister quite seriously although he had often thought that Vanessa showed more concern and protective instincts towards her sisters.

Fiona's eyes brightened at his suggestion and she hurried to the telephone. Justin found Rowena in the garden with John Byfield and interrupted their idyll without a qualm to ask the girl if Belinda had hinted that she might not be back that evening. Rowena knew nothing, seemed surprised to hear that her sisters had not returned, brushed aside the necessity for anxiety and was obviously impatient at the interruption. Justin went in search of Melissa . . . was easily guided to her by the sound of piano music. She was in the drawing-room, playing softly, while Raif Fitzgerald lounged by the fireplace and watched her with his heart in his eyes for all to see. Justin apologised for the interruption, put the same questions and received much the same answers. But Melissa immediately left the piano and turned to Raif so instinctively with the suggestion that they might go to look for them that Justin knew that it would not be long before his shrewd perception was proved right. They took Raif's car and drove off into the dark, assuring Fiona as they left that they would undoubtedly meet the girls on their way back from Town.

Raif's car passed the new and increasingly popular roadhouse just as a sudden influx of cars arrived and blocked their view of the pale blue coupé in the grounds . . . and a few minutes later Vanessa and Belinda came out, got into the car and began the last stage of their journey home.

The sound of the car in the drive brought Justin to the door. The heady relief that swept over him as he saw both girls, safe and sound in evident high spirits, swiftly turned to a fierce anger for their lack of thought.

'Where the devil have you been?' he confronted them.

Belinda stared at him, tilting her chin. 'Is that your business?'

Vanessa felt a cold hand grip her heart. 'Is anything wrong . . . Fiona, the girls?' she asked on a surge of anxiety.

'They're fine . . . we weren't so sure about you,' he told her, tight-lipped. 'Why didn't you telephone? You were expected back to dinner—or had you forgotten?'

'Oh . . . !' Vanessa flushed. 'We didn't think . . .'

'You empty-headed pair of fools!' he snapped. 'We almost had the police scouring the roads for you.'

'Don't tell me *you* were worried about us,' Belinda sneered, stepping out of the car.

'That's unimportant,' he retorted. 'Fiona has been half out of her mind with worry. She insisted that you would have telephoned if you meant to be late. I was stupid enough to believe that she knew what she was talking about . . . that she knew Vanessa better than I did and that if she hadn't telephoned something must have happened to you both!'

Vanessa looked at his taut, angry face—and her heart sank. For a brief period of time, she had been able to put her unhappiness to the back of her mind. Faced with his anger and contempt, misconstruing the depth of feeling behind it, she realised the hopelessness of loving a man who did not welcome their safe return with open arms and a glad heart. His concern was all for Fiona who had been needlessly worried and although it indicated that he was capable of compassion and warm feeling and consideration, it seemed that Fiona was the one who had broken through the barrier of his antagonism and not the woman he had kissed in the shadows and who loved him so desperately . . .

'All that happened was that I became engaged,' Belinda told him pertly and flashed the big ring on her finger. 'We decided to celebrate—that's why we're late.'

'Congratulations,' he said curtly and insincerely. He could not be bothered with Belinda's engagement at such a time. He did not even feel surprise. He turned on Vanessa. 'And did you get engaged too? Is that why you never gave Fiona a thought when you decided to celebrate?'

She bit her lip at the heavy sarcasm in his tone. 'No . . .' she said quietly. 'I'm sorry . . . it was thoughtless but the unexpectedness of Belinda's news drove everything out of my head.'

'Well, you'd better come in and explain to Fiona.' He walked into the house abruptly.

'I don't know why you let him talk to you like that,' Belinda said, outraged. 'Why don't you give him as good as you get?'

Vanessa made a slight gesture of weary helplessness. 'There's enough hostility in this house without adding to it,' she said quietly . . . and went in to comfort and apologise to Fiona whose relief, in this case, had turned to thankful tears and self-mocking laughter. There was the news of Belinda's engagement to rouse her from near-hysteria—and eager

191

questions and explanations and amused incredulity filled the room with a babble of sound.

Vanessa studied Justin as he stood by the window with a drink in his hand, his dark eyes inscrutable as his gaze flitted from one to other of the Clements. His anger had died but left him with a smouldering resentment that Vanessa's thoughtlessness had caused him to betray the depth of his feelings before others. It did not occur to him that she had taken his fury at its face value, that she was blind to the naked anguish of relief and love in his eyes, that she merely thought that his opinion of her was even lower, if possible, than it had been before.

Their eyes met across the room. Vanessa glanced away hastily and turned to speak to Raif who, with Melissa, had returned to Fairlands a few minutes before after a fruitless search of the main arterial road from Town. She was deeply regretful that her lack of thought had caused so much concern . . . and warmed by the thought that Fiona and her younger sisters should be so fond of herself and Belinda that they had been filled with anxiety when they had not returned when expected.

Justin longed to cross the room, to dismiss Raif, to draw Vanessa to him and pour out the mingled emotions which fought so turbulently within him. But she had turned from his gaze so pointedly that he knew it would be foolish to risk the humiliation of a snub. He finished his drink and went quietly from the room . . . and Vanessa watched him go unhappily.

CHAPTER FOURTEEN

Vanessa sat at the big, highly-polished desk, piled with its evidence of the work that had occupied so much of Justin's time in the last few weeks. A faint smile touched her lips as she ran her fingers lightly, lovingly over the polished wood and thought of him sitting at the desk, his dark head bowed over the papers, a frown of concentration creasing his forehead. The room was imbued with his warm, masculine personality and she allowed herself to dream that everything was different, that there had never been that fierce hostility between them, that they had formed an easy friendship on sight . . . a friendship which had slowly ripened into mutual love.

Justin walked into the study with a book in his hand. He was taken aback to find Vanessa at his desk—or, rather, Byfield's desk now, he thought grimly. He threw her a curious glance.

Vanessa leaped to her feet and moved towards the door, feeling guilty and embarrassed at being found at his desk.

'Don't run away,' he said smoothly. 'I only came to return a book.' He was puzzled by the strange, hunted, almost guilty expression in her eyes. Much as she might dislike him, did she have to rush from a room the moment he entered it, did she have to avoid him as though he were a leper, did she have to be stricken dumb whenever she encountered him. At the end of the week, he was leaving Fairlands . . . was he to take the memory of antagonism, resentment and harsh words with him? Couldn't they talk together like reasonable human beings just once before he left?

'I promised Belinda I'd . . .'

'Damn Belinda!' he said forcefully.

Her eyes flashed swiftly. 'That's typical. That's just what you'd like to do, isn't it? Damn Belinda and every one of us to hell!'

Amusement flooded him at that swift, protective anger in defence of her sister. His eyes crinkled with laughter and he said unsteadily: 'How well you know me . . . considering we never exchange two words but we squabble like a couple of spoiled children.'

Vanessa looked at him doubtfully but she could not resist the infectious twinkle in his eyes. An unexpected friendliness seemed to emanate from him and she felt a smile tugging at her mouth in instinctive response. 'It's true . . .' she said, clinging to the shreds of her annoyance.

He spread his hands helplessly. 'Do you really blame me, Vanessa? You must admit that all of you are damned hard to handle . . . and much too quick to take offence.'

'You usually mean to be offensive,' she said tartly.

'We rub each other the wrong way,' he defended.

'You set out to be unpleasant from the start,' she retorted swiftly.

Justin laughed again. 'Here we go again! Vanessa, couldn't we try not to be at loggerheads all the time?'

'There isn't much time left,' she said, an unconscious regret stealing into her voice.

Justin looked at her thoughtfully. 'No . . . we have left it rather late to cry pax.'

'Do you really want to?' she taunted. 'I don't know why you should suddenly feel guilty about turning Fairlands into a battle-field . . . it seems to me that you've enjoyed every minute of it!'

He smiled. 'Perhaps I have . . . where you're concerned.'

She looked up at him quickly. 'Why me?'

'You're so fiery when you're roused . . . and I hate to see you looking so wretched when you're not. I feel that I must do something to chase that look from your eyes—if it's only to goad you into an argument.'

His voice held so much tender concern that sudden tears sprang to her eyes. 'Why should you care if I'm unhappy?'

He shrugged. 'I don't know why you should be, my dear—haven't you got everything you ever wanted?'

She turned on him fiercely. 'Oh, you fool! When did I ever want to turn you out of your home and take Fairlands from you . . . or want to leave the place where I was happy because the girls needed me and we were close to come to this beastly house where the servants treat us as if we were cockroaches and you show your contempt for us in every word? I hate Fairlands and I don't want the money—and I wish my mother hadn't been one of the royal Fairgarths!' Tears streamed down her cheeks and her mouth quivered as the words tumbled from her lips in a torrent of emotion.

Justin reached her in one stride and drew her into his arms. 'Whoa! there . . . steady on my girl,' he said.

Vanessa buried her face in his shoulder and gave herself up to the reassurance of his arms. 'And I'd rather you flew at me than talked to me as though I were a temperamental mare!' she stormed tempestuously. Then she raised her head and stared at him suspiciously as his body shook with laughter.

'Oh, my darling . . . I do love you!' he said exultantly and then, on a lower, gentler note:

'I love you very much . . . and I'll try to remember that you're not a temperamental mare in future.'

The colour fled from her face as she saw all the love, all the naked need, all the tenderness in his eyes. 'How can you?' she asked unsteadily. 'I've been hateful to you.'

'And I've been hateful to you . . . but only because I loved you so much and you made me so angry because you wouldn't pause for a moment from quarrelling to give me the chance to show it. I can't help thinking that everyone but you knows how I feel about you.' He hugged her suddenly. 'People only fight like that when they love each other, my darling,' he told her indulgently.

She searched his eyes wonderingly. 'Then you knew why I've been so miserable?'

'Not until you flew at me just now . . . and put my feelings before your own. I never realised you felt so deeply about my loss of Fairlands. Oh, Vanessa, what a lot of time we've wasted . . .' He caught her close, tilting her chin with his hand, smiling into her eyes with all his love glowing in his own eyes before he touched her eager, willing, incredibly sweet lips with his own . . . and Vanessa forgot everything but the joy of realising that her love had not been in vain, after all . . .

Madison coughed discreetly and they leaped apart. 'Excuse me, Mr. Justin—

Madam. A lady insists on seeing you—a Mrs. Cornelius Packer. She won't tell me her business. Shall I ask her to wait in the drawing-room?'

'Er . . . no, ask her to come in here, will you, Madison.' As the butler withdrew, he turned to Vanessa and touched her cheek with a gentle finger. 'I'd better deal with the lady and then I can concentrate on asking you to marry me,' he said gently.

She was radiant in her new-found happiness. 'It can wait for half an hour now,' she told him happily. 'I'd better go and find Belinda.'

'No, don't go, darling,' he said urgently as he caught sight of a stout, bejewelled, imposing figure in full sail towards the study. 'I might need your moral support—whatever Mrs. Cornelius Packer wants with me.' He turned with a smile to greet his visitor. 'Mrs. Packer . . . I'm Justin Fairgarth. I understand you want to see me?'

Her small, bright eyes narrowed as she studied him for a long moment without speaking. Then she said cheerily: 'So you're Justin . . . well, you've grown a bit since I last saw you, lad. You don't take after your father . . . more like my side of the family.' Then, at his obvious bewilderment: 'Eh, but you don't know what I'm talking about, do you? I was always one to rush my fences. Let me sit down, lad—I carry a lot of weight and the good Lord never thought to provide me with a pair of substantial feet.'

Justin hastily pulled forward a chair. Vanessa said uncertainly: 'Justin, I think you'll want to have a private conversation with Mrs. Packer.'

'Is this your wife, Justin?' She looked her up and down appraisingly, kindly.

He was completely at a loss. 'Not yet,' he said with a swift, comprehensive glance for Vanessa.

'You're going to be married? Well, that *is* nice!' She settled herself more comfortably in the chair. 'What's your name, dear?' She was slightly vulgar and yet oddly appealing . . . Vanessa thought her a comfortable, motherly type and liked her readily but she was completely bewildered by the meaning remarks she had made about Justin.

'Vanessa Clement,' she said, smiling.

'Pretty—but then so are you. So was I when I was your age . . . although you might not think it now. Justin's father thought so . . .'

Justin broke in on the faintly reminiscent note of her words. 'Am I to understand that you claim to be my . . . well, my mother, Mrs. Packer?' he asked bluntly.

She nodded. 'Quick on the uptake,' she said proudly. 'Yes, I'm your mother, lad . . . I hope I don't put you out by coming here like this? I only came over from the States last week . . . Mr. Packer's an American business-man and very happy we've been, to be sure. Never a moment's worry and faithful as the day is long . . . and *he's* not ashamed to call me his wife. Still, I admit it wouldn't have been easy for Wilfrid with his stuck-up family to spring someone like me on them.'

'Wilfrid!' The exclamation was forced from Justin in astonishment and Vanessa caught her breath sharply. 'You can't mean that my uncle . . .'

'Not your uncle, lad—your father,' she told him with a noticeable air of triumph.

'I see,' Justin said quietly. He was completely stunned by this surprising revelation—could scarcely believe this stout, rather common stranger had ever been a part of his austere, brusque uncle's life.

'Oh, it was legal enough,' she told him firmly, sensing a faint disapproval in his tone. She rummaged in her capacious handbag. 'I've got the papers here . . . all of them. I've always kept them and thankful now that I did. As soon as I heard that poor Wilfrid was dead and that everything he owned had gone to his nieces, I knew it was my duty to put things right.' She found the papers and thrust them towards him. 'It's all right and tight, lad. Wilfrid married me when he found out that you were on the way—not that I wanted marriage but it made things easier, I will admit.'

Justin glanced at the papers, his expression very grave . . . the marriage certificate, his own birth certificate and a decree of divorce. 'You were divorced?'

'I met a nice young fellow, one of my own kind, who'd been a trouper since he was a kid. We did the halls together and he wanted to marry me. I'd never lived with Wilfrid—his family never knew about me nor his posh friends either, come to that. I suppose he was ashamed of marrying a chorus girl.' She preened herself unexpectedly. 'In the chorus at the Collodeum, I was—and very good, too, though I says it myself. Had to give it up when you were on the way but I got a job with a touring company after you were born and that's where I met Albert. He was a good man, my Albert,' she added with easy tears brimming on her heavily-mascaraed lashes. 'I missed him when he went.'

'He died?' Vanessa asked gently.

'Lord love you, no! Ran off with the producer's wife! Silly little thing . . . not much sense but Albert wanted her and I wouldn't stand in their way. I went to New York to try my luck there and that's when I met Mr. Packer . . . and never regretted it.' She beamed at Justin. 'I've not come to make any claims on you, lad . . . we don't know each other. I've barely given you a thought since you were a baby and I expect Wilfrid did the right thing by you. I don't know the

201

ins and outs of this business about his house and his money—but I thought that if he went without leaving a will and no one knew that you were his heir, then you'd be pushed out of your rightful heritage. I haven't done much for you Justin . . . but I can put that right, at least.'

'That's exactly what did happen,' Vanessa told her impulsively. She slipped her hand into Justin's arm. 'Oh, I am glad, Justin! Fairlands *is* yours, you see . . . I always felt it should be.'

'I feel rather staggered,' he admitted frankly. Suddenly he smiled at the woman who claimed to be his mother. 'But I'm grateful to you, Mrs. Packer.'

'I told Cornelius it was the right thing to do. He advised me not to interfere—said Wilfrid wasn't likely to have died without leaving a will and that he must have meant his nieces to inherit everything. I didn't know if I'd find you here but I knew someone would be able to tell me where you were.' She looked about the luxurious, comfortable room. 'So this is Fairlands . . . Wilfrid was always talking about it when we were courting. I'd like to have a good look over the place,' she said wistfully. 'I never had the chance to live here and heaven knows I'd have been stifled in the country . . . but I always wanted to look over it.'

'I hope you and your husband will come

and stay as my guests for a time before you go back to America,' Justin said swiftly.

'Now that *is* kind!' she exclaimed warmly. 'I must say Cornelius will be delighted . . . he's very interested in old English houses. But I don't want to be a nuisance to you, lad. I didn't come to force a mother on you . . . only to help you.'

'You have helped me immensely—and I shall always be grateful,' he told her quietly. 'Of course, these certificates will have to be checked and proved before I can claim Fairlands and that will take time. But I'm hoping to get married and have an extended honeymoon,' he added with a smile for Vanessa.

Mrs. Packer clambered to her feet. 'Well, I've done what I came to do and I'll take myself off now.' She held out her hand to Vanessa. 'I like you, dear,' she said frankly. 'I think you're well suited to my boy—and I hope you'll be very happy.'

'You'll stay and have lunch with us,' Justin said impulsively.

'No . . . not this time, Justin,' she said firmly. 'Mr. Packer is waiting in the car and I've promised to visit an old church in the neighbourhood with him.' She brought out an envelope from her bag. 'Here's my address . . . the Savoy Hotel.' She chuckled. 'I never thought I'd stay at the Savoy! Your lawyers will want to get in touch with me.'

'So will I,' he assured her warmly and stooped to touch her heavily-powdered, fleshy cheek with his lips. She coloured and thrust a flimsy lace handkerchief to her nose, blew mightily, gulped and then waddled towards the door.

Justin went with her, kept her in conversation for a few minutes in the hall, helped her into the car, shook hands with Cornelius Packer, a timid little man who did not look in the least like a successful business-man and seemed highly embarrassed at the introduction, watched the car until it turned out of the gates and then hurried back to Vanessa who was looking through the certificates.

She turned to him eagerly. 'Oh, Justin . . . how wonderful! It must be true?'

'I don't know . . . those look genuine enough,' he said, indicating the papers on his desk. 'Vanessa, I can't believe it myself . . . it seems too fantastic—and why didn't Uncle Wilfrid tell me the truth years ago.'

'Perhaps he'd thought of you as his nephew for so long that he'd quite forgotten you were really his son,' she suggested.

'No,' he said slowly. 'I expect he thought that there was plenty of time . . .' He caught her into his arms and tilted her chin so that he could look into her eyes. 'You really are glad? You don't mind . . . you and your sisters will lose the income you were already taking for granted.'

Vanessa laughed shakily. 'I never took it for granted!'

'No, you haven't touched your share of the income,' he remembered.

'I'm afraid the girls have made quite a hole in *your* income, though,' she reminded him.

'They're welcome to it . . . and they needn't worry about the future. After all, I'll be their brother-in-law as well as their cousin and I can't allow them to starve!'

She strained on tiptoes to reach his lips, brushed them lightly with her own. 'Don't you think we've talked too much already about the whole business?' she asked softly, teasingly . . . and caught her breath for sheer happiness as his arms tightened about her and she knew again the sweet, thrilling wonder of his kiss while the word turned unheeded and they lived in their own private world of love.

Photoset, printed and bound in Great Britain by
REDWOOD BURN LIMITED, Trowbridge, Wiltshire